BOOK TW

MUST COLLINWOOD AGAIN KNOW DEATH AND DESTRUCTION?

Ann Hayward, a beautiful bride honeymooning at Collinwood, is fearful that her husband, John, is losing his mind and wants to kill her. Time after time, she barely survives the attempts on her life, until she finally turns to Barnabas with her problem.

Barnabas, knowing the evil that prevails at Collinwood, does not think that John is the would-be assassin, and searches elsewhere for the answer.

Eric Collins, whom Ann has rejected as a suitor, is a suspect, as is Simeon Hal, who wants to avenge John Hayward for an imagined wrong. Even Warren Miller, the masked recluse living on the estate, is a possibility.

Will Ann Hayward meet a gruesome death somewhere in the shadowy secret passages of the old mansion? Or will Barnabas be able to stop the murderer—and a great peril to all of Collinwood—before it is too late?

Hermes Press

Published by Hermes Press, an imprint of
Herman and Geer Communications, Inc.

Daniel Herman, Publisher
Troy Musguire, Production Manager
Eileen Sabrina Herman, Managing Editor
Alissa Fisher, Graphic Design
Kandice Hartner, Senior Editor

2100 Wilmington Road
Neshannock, Pennsylvania 16105
(724) 652-0511
www.HermesPress.com; info@hermespress.com

Book design by Eileen Sabrina Herman
First printing, 2021

LCCN applied for: 10 9 8 7 6 5 4 3 2 1 0
ISBN 978-1-61345-241-7
OCR and text editing by H + G Media and Eileen Sabrina Herman
Proof reading by Eileen Sabrina Herman and Feytaline McKinley

From Dan, Sabrina, and Jacob in memory of Al DeVivo

Acknowledgments: This book would not be possible without the help and
encouragement of Jim Pierson and Curtis Holdings

Barnabas, Quentin and the Frightened Bride
by Marilyn Ross

CONTENTS

CHAPTER 1

It was late afternoon of an October day and Carolyn had gone up to the lookout tower atop Collinwood to enjoy the panoramic view from it. Her mother, Elizabeth, had suggested she should and told her of the flaming beauty of the maples on the estate as seen from up there. Now Carolyn paused by the railing of the small, ornately-constructed tower and gazed down at the grounds and the area beyond.

The stately mansion of Collinwood had stood on this Maine cliff, which dominated Collinsport Bay, for many years. From where she watched, Carolyn could see the distant town of Collinsport on a point to her left and the Collinsport lighthouse on a barren rock far out towards the ocean on her right. In the sheltered area of the bay between these points many pleasure craft sailed during the summer months. Just now the bay was deserted except for a few of the fishing boats that operated in conjunction with the fish packing plant owned by her family.

Collinwood had beauty in every season of the year. Now, clad in the gaudy colors of autumn foliage, it offered an especially pleasant sight. The sun had a golden, waning hue and there was a stirring of melancholy in the air. Though this brief period of special loveliness heralded the approaching winter, for the moment, it had a royal splendor.

Only recently, Barnabas Collins had left the estate to return to England or wherever he made up his mind to go during the winter. The departure of this handsome British cousin of the family had made her sad as it always had, from her earliest memories as a child. Barnabas, with his charm and dignified manner, brought a special something to the group. She only wished that he would one day decide to remain there for the entire year rather than just pay occasional visits. But he was a wanderer by nature and did not like to remain anywhere long.

She couldn't help wishing he was there with her to share the lovely view from this vantage spot. It was breathtakingly beautiful. Now, along the road which followed the cliffs and led from the main highway to the estate, there speeded a sleek gray sedan. She studied the progress of the car as it came nearer to Collinwood and decided it must be the reporter from the Ellsworth paper who, earlier in the day, had phoned her mother with a request for an interview.

The reporter aroused the curiosity of both Carolyn and her mother. He gave no hint of what he wanted to talk to Elizabeth Stoddard about, other than saying it had to do with the history of the village. Anxious to be downstairs when this visitor arrived, Carolyn quickly left the lookout tower to go below.

When she reached the lower hallway, she saw her mother seated in the large, elegantly furnished living room on the right. She went in and told her, "The reporter is on his way. I saw him when I was up in the tower."

Elizabeth glanced up with a smile. "Good. I'll be glad to get it over with and have him on his way. If your Uncle Roger arrives home and finds him here, he'll start complaining."

Carolyn sighed. "What makes Uncle Roger so difficult?"

"We have had problems with the press about family matters," Elizabeth admitted. "I suppose that has made him sensitive. But I believe the young man on the phone said this had to do with the history of Collinsport."

"We'll soon know," Carolyn said with a gleam of excitement in her eyes.

At the same instant a car came to a halt in the driveway before the old mansion and a young man in a tan trench coat got out and came up to the door. He'd barely pressed the bell when Carolyn opened the door to him.

He was twentyish, sandy-haired, and had a round, pleasant face. "I'm Jim Mason from the Ellsworth Journal," he said. "I'm expected."

"I know," she said, with a smile for him in return. She liked his clean-cut looks and manner. "Mother is waiting for you in the living room." She showed him in.

Elizabeth rose to greet him. "My daughter, Carolyn, and I have been quite intrigued since your phone call, trying to guess what you wanted to discuss with me."

He smiled politely. "I hadn't intended to sound mysterious."

"But you did," Elizabeth insisted. "Your vague references to the history of the village could mean anything." She waved him to an easy chair. "Please do sit down."

"Thank you," he said.

Carolyn and her mother sat on a divan directly opposite him. Carolyn asked, "Are you a native of this part of Maine, Mr. Mason?"

"No," he said, his eyes showing a twinkle. "I'm from Vermont, but I've always had a desire to work by the ocean. The chance to come here was too good to resist."

Elizabeth laughed. "This is as close to the ocean as you can get."

"I know it." He glanced around with interest. "I won't deny I was anxious to come out here and see you. I've heard so much about Collinwood... this is my first time on the estate."

"What are your impressions?" Carolyn wanted to know.

He considered. "I don't believe I've any really clear-cut ones yet. I had a lot of preconceived ideas about the place. I guess you are aware it has a kind of reputation as a haunted mansion."

Elizabeth nodded. "Any house a hundred years old or more is bound to have legends grow up around it."

"That is true," the reporter said seriously. "And Collinwood is no exception. I've gone through the file on the estate and the number of eerie ghost tales associated with it is amazing."

"I've grown up with them," Carolyn said, with a tiny sigh.

"And yet I find both the house and location charming rather than spooky," Jim said.

"Thank you," Elizabeth said. "But then, on this charming autumn afternoon you are seeing it at its best. Perhaps you should be here when the wind is blowing in from the ocean and it is pouring rain."

"That's when the shutters rattle, the house creaks and phantoms peer in the rain-lashed windows," Carolyn teased.

He took it in good part. "That sounds more in character with the Collinwood I've heard about."

"There is such a Collinwood," Carolyn's mother assured him. "The place would be lacking if it had no such legends. We treasure our ghosts and demons here as other estates take pride in their lawns and gardens. The weird tales about this house have made it famous."

The young reporter gave her an enquiring glance. "And you don't resent them?"

"Not really," Elizabeth said. "Some of them are founded on true cases of haunting. I don't deny the existence of a supernatural."

"Few intelligent people do," the young man said seriously as he took a notebook from his pocket. "I'm afraid my business here today is of an extremely prosaic nature. It has nothing to do with your celebrated history of vampires, werewolves and other assorted monsters."

"Please tell us quickly what it is you are here to find out," Carolyn pleaded. "I'm dying of curiosity."

He laughed. "Forgive me," he said. And then, consulting his notebook again, he addressed himself to her mother. "What can you tell me about Nursing Sister Ann Hayward?"

Elizabeth gave him a strange look. "The frightened bride," she said, almost to herself, speaking in a low voice.

The young reporter looked puzzled. "What is that, Mrs. Stoddard?"

"Nothing," she said, at once casual again. "What is it you wish to know about Ann Hayward?"

"You'll recall the hospital has an Ann Hayward wing. I believe she donated the money for it some years back."

"Yes," Elizabeth nodded. "In the early nineteen-twenties when the hospital was being built."

"Exactly," the reporter said. "Right now the hospital is being renovated and enlarged, and the Ann Hayward wing is being rebuilt though the Haywards are no longer here in Collinsport."

"No," Elizabeth said. "The Wetmore family bought their big house and use it only as a summer place these days."

"So I understand," he said. "I haven't been able to discover whether any of the Hayward family are living and where they are. I want to do a story on this nurse who gave such a generous donation to the original hospital and had that wing dedicated to her. I hoped you might be able to tell me something about her."

Elizabeth smiled sadly. "I can give you some information, though not all of it may be interesting. My family knew her well. If you'll excuse me for a moment. I'll get some newspaper clippings I've collected about her." And with that, she left the room.

The young man turned his attention to Carolyn. "I had an idea Collinwood was filled with old ghost-ridden people," he confessed. "I wasn't expecting to find anyone as young as you."

"There are some younger," she assured him. "My cousin, David, and a little girl who is staying here, named Amy."

He gave her a searching look. "Have you ever seen any ghosts here?"

"Everyone has," she admitted. "On foggy nights you can almost sense their presence. I haven't seen any particular one, but

I've been faced with doors that slammed for no reason, I've seen the curtains at windows billow as if by phantom hands and I've heard low moanings that I haven't been able to explain. For the really frightening stories you should talk to our cousin, Barnabas Collins."

The reporter's face showed·interest. "Of course, Barnabas Collins! I've heard about him. He's rather a way-out character, isn't he? I mean, if you'll excuse me for being frank, nothing disrespectful meant."

She smiled grimly. "Barnabas is a wonderful, charming man."

"Sounds as if he must be to have you say so as sincerely as that." The young man sounded impressed. "I've heard that he wears those latest mod London clothes, the Edwardian caped-coat and string tie. He also keeps to himself a lot. Isn't he an artist or writer, or something?"

"He's writing a family history and when he's here he lives at what we call the old house. It's on the road to the cemetery."

"That's something else I've heard," the reporter said. "That this Barnabas likes to roam around cemeteries at night. Is that true?"

"He does enjoy the atmosphere of old places—including cemeteries," she said. "But to picture him as a kind of ghoul is an exaggeration. He's cultured and nice."

"I'll take your word for it and not listen to any more gossip," he promised.

Carolyn was almost indignant. "I think you'd be wise to do just that. I know there are wild stories about his being a vampire. It's hard to believe what some people will accept as gospel."

"I've been in the newspaper business long enough to know that," he said. "Thanks for setting me straight about your cousin. Any chance of me seeing him while I'm here?"

She shook her head. "I'm afraid not. He's just left for England."

"Too bad," he said, disappointed. "I'm sure I could have managed a good story on him."

"He'll be back again later," she said. "You can interview him then."

"I must," he agreed.

Elizabeth returned with several snapshots and some yellowed newspaper clippings and gave them to Jim Mason, saying, "These may be of some help. That's a snapshot of Ann and her husband, John. They returned here after the First World War. He was in the army and injured at the battle of Belleau Wood. She was the English nurse who took care of him. They fell in love and married, and then returned here to build a house—the Hayward family mansion had burned down while John was away."

The reporter looked up from the snapshots with interest.

"You seem to know all about what went on."

"Most of it," she said with a faint smile. "While the young people were waiting for their house to be built they lived here at Collinwood."

"Here?" he questioned.

"In this very house," she said. "William Collins was the squire of Collinwood in 1920. He was a widower and had one son, Eric, whose twin brother was struck down by some weird wasting disease. They took him to Boston for treatment but he didn't respond. He died before they could get him home. Because of that, William Collins was a very indulgent father and spoiled Eric, allowing him to waste his time and drink too much."

Carolyn listened to her mother with amazement. "You've never told me any of this!"

Her mother smiled. "I guess we've never gone into the family history of that period," she said. "It was a strange, though exciting era, I understand. All the young people then were trying to start new lives for themselves after years of war—a war that ended with the founding of the League of Nations. The League was supposed to bring us peace for all time, after the war to end wars."

"And it didn't work out that way," Carolyn said wryly.

"I'm afraid not," Elizabeth sighed. "Can either of you young people even tell me who was our President at that time? People are forgotten so easily!"

"President Woodrow Wilson?" Carolyn hazarded.

The young reporter spoke up. "I think it would have been President Harding by the time the Haywards arrived back here. You said this John Hayward was in the hospital for a time after the war."

"You're right," Elizabeth smiled. "President Harding was in office during the time the Haywards lived in this house. You saw few automobiles around Collinsport then, but there were plenty of horses and carriages, and the young men wore straw hats and the girls had just started cutting their hair short and wearing hideous long dresses."

"Didn't the dresses get shorter soon afterward?" Carolyn wanted to know.

"You're right," Elizabeth said. "The hemline kept going up until by the late twenties the skirts were almost as short as the mini-skirts are now."

"Great!" Jim sounded amused. "I'm getting a history of American styles along with the story of Ann Hayward."

"I've digressed," Elizabeth apologized. "To go back to the Haywards, the house was finished but that poor bride and groom never did live in it. He died and she felt so sad she decided to return to her native London. But before she went she gave the hospital enough money for the wing that was dedicated in her name."

"I'll be able to get the information I want from these clippings," the reporter said. "I'm certainly obliged to you."

"I'm glad to help," Elizabeth said. "But I would appreciate your sending the clippings and snapshots back to me. My cousin, Barnabas, is writing a family history and he'll undoubtedly want these for references one day."

"I promise I'll return them," Jim said. With a special smile for Carolyn, he added, "I'll return them myself, if I may, and perhaps you'll show me some of the famous spots around here, such as Widows' Hill and the cemetery?"

Carolyn blushed. "I'd enjoy doing that."

"Come back any time," Elizabeth said warmly.

Carolyn showed him to the front door. "When is the story appearing in the paper?" she asked.

"In a week or so," he said. "We're only a weekly, you know."

"I should," she smiled. "I've been reading the paper all my life."

He laughed. "I keep forgetting I'm the stranger here."

"Try and get back in the daytime. It will be easier to show you around," Carolyn said.

"Would a Sunday afternoon be all right?"

"Ideal."

"Great," he said, with an admiring look. "You people have been wonderful to me. Your mother is very nice."

"I think so," she said.

"And so are you," he added quickly. "I'll be giving you a call this Sunday or the next." With a final smile and a wave, he left.

Carolyn watched for a minute and then went inside. Her mother looked amused. "You and that young man got along wonderfully," she said.

"He's a nice boy."

"I think so, too," Elizabeth said. "I wish him luck with his story." She turned and started up the broad stairway.

"Mother!" Carolyn called after her.

Elizabeth turned on the stairway. "Yes?"

"I listened while you told him about Ann Hayward, and I don't think you told him the whole story."

Her mother arched an eyebrow. "How discerning you're becoming these days!"

"It's true, isn't it? You did keep something back."

"Perhaps," her mother said.

"I must hear all of it," she begged.

"Later."

"When?"

"I certainly haven't time now. It will take quite a while." Elizabeth gave her an indulgent smile. "Come to my room at bedtime—I'll tell you then."

"I'd like that," Carolyn exulted. "It will be something like when I was a little girl and you told me bedtime stories."

"That's hardly an apt comparison," Elizabeth said dryly. "You'll find this bedtime story rather more exciting than the ones you used to make me tell you."

"I'll come to your room around ten-thirty," Carolyn promised.

"Very well," Elizabeth said. "And don't bother me anymore about this just now. I have to see to dinner."

The matter was dropped for the time being, but Carolyn did not forget it. She looked forward to the true facts about Ann Hayward with a feeling of tense excitement. During the evening, she looked up everything she could find about the nineteen-twenties. It was a new world to her.

As night fell, a high wind rose. By the time Carolyn went to her mother's room, the old house was creaking and groaning in its best ghostly fashion. The lonely wind really set the mood for the story.

Elizabeth smiled as she entered. "I thought you might forget my promise and not come."

"That was hardly likely," Carolyn said. "I've been dying to hear all about Nursing Sister Ann Hayward."

"Make yourself comfortable on the foot of the bed," her mother advised. "It's quite a long story."

Carolyn snuggled up comfortably on the bed and her mother sat down in an easy chair.

"I hardly know where to begin," Elizabeth confessed. "I suppose the best place would be the night Ann and John Hayward arrived here. They had already sent word ahead to start the building of their new house. William Collins met them at the railway depot with his carriage that warm June evening. Ann had no idea then that she was about to enter on a time of terror that would make all her war experiences fade into nothingness, and that for her, Collinwood would become a place she'd always remember with fear. Indeed, those that lived here then came to speak of her as the frightened bride."

"The frightened bride," Carolyn echoed in a small, tense voice.

The lights in the bedroom seemed to dim and the lonely October wind pressed hard against the windows, making them rattle as if they were being tapped by the bony fingers of phantoms. And then the wind faded with a weird sighing sound as if in mourning for those long ago lost times...

Ann Hayward sat very straight on the uncomfortable horsehair seat as the carriage creaked and bumped over the rough road. Except for the pale moon that beamed down on the narrow country road in ghostly fashion, there was no light and William Collins apparently did not feel his carriage required a lantern on it. Ann could only dimly see their host-to-be sitting across from her in the near darkness, his hands clasped on the head of the cane he held firmly in front of him.

She had only briefly glimpsed his stern, angular face at the railway station. He appeared to be a good man, but surely aloof and grim. His behavior thus far had borne that out. He sat in silence when a few words on his part might have put her more at ease. She would have welcomed any friendliness. She was a stranger in a strange land with a husband, who was seated at her side, who was anything but well.

A gentle look crossed her delicate, oval face as she turned to glance at the fine profile of John Hayward. He was staring straight ahead, as if lost in his thoughts. She was used to these silent spells which came fairly often. Her large gray eyes took on a soft gleam as she recalled her first meeting with him when he was a patient in a hospital devoted to wounded members of the Expeditionary Forces.

Her chestnut hair had been almost concealed by her nursing headdress which flowed down over her shoulders but somehow he had noticed it. Looking up at her from his pillow with hollow-eyed wonder, he'd murmured, "I like the combination of your hair and eyes. You're lovely!"

Ann had heard a number of compliments from the young men she'd taken care of in army hospitals. They had become routine to her. But there was something in the way this noble-looking, dark-haired American phrased his tribute that touched her. Quietly, she'd said, "Thank you. I'm glad to know you, John Hayward."

"What's your name?" he'd asked.

"Ann, Ann Forester," she said as she studied his emaciated face, saddened to think of one so young here in this ward devoted to cases of the shell-shocked.

"Ann Forester," he'd repeated. "It's a nice name, and just looking at you makes me feel better."

That had been the start of the romance that had resulted in their marriage. Ann had known what she might be letting herself in for. She'd worked the night shifts when nightmares and the terrors of battle came to those piteous shell shock victims. She'd stood by as John writhed in his bed, tortured by fantasies beyond her comprehension. She'd seen the moments of trembling overcome him, and moments when he'd appeared not quite sane. Her heart had gone out to him, with the single desire to save him from the stupid cruelty which any war signified for her. Perhaps her love for him was based on her anguish for all those broken young bodies she'd attended as a nurse.

And John Hayward had responded to her warm affection and his recovery had been remarkable, contrasted with some of the others in the ward. Yet there was a dark side to their new-found happiness. It was essential that John be protected from undue tension and the clamor of a city, and Ann had to rent a cottage for them in Essex. There they had lived a quiet, pleasant existence for several months, until John had become restless, anxious to return to America and his home village of Collinsport.

From him she'd learned about the Maine village and its people. Together, they worked on the plans for their new home, which he mailed ahead so the work could be started. It was decided that while they were waiting for the house to be completed, they would live with his friends at Collinwood.

"You'll like the old mansion," he promised her. "It will be quiet, too. William Collins lives there with his son, Eric, and a few servants. His wife died many years ago and he lost Thomas, Eric's twin, about five years ago. He had always been the sturdy, athletic one and then he was stricken by some wasting disease."

"How horrible!" she said.

John nodded. "I only saw him once after his illness. He had changed almost beyond recognition. He didn't seem to recognize me at all. They took him to Boston for treatment but he never returned. Since then, William Collins has doted on the remaining twin, Eric, to Eric's disadvantage, since he is a wild character given to drinking and general carousing. But in his father's eyes he can do no wrong."

"You're sure we won't be imposing on the Collins family?" she queried.

"Not at all. William has written he'll be delighted to have us," her husband assured her.

Ann had looked forward to living in America but then some dark moments had come to shadow their pleasant times in the Essex cottage. John had suffered a mild setback and again he was tortured by grim nightmares. One night, in his delirium, he turned on her and attempted to strangle her. She'd barely managed to loosen the grip of those mad, vice-like fingers from her throat and scream to him to make him come out of his demented state.

Incidents like this occurred twice more before they left the cottage for the journey to America. They left permanent scars on her mind. She'd begun to worry if the husband she loved would ever fully recover. It was too soon after the war to know—too soon for the doctors to have learned enough about this particular psychosis from the other shattered victims. The hospital wards were still crowded with prematurely white-haired young men with wide, frightened eyes and the palsied hands that were the marks of their torture. For them the horrors of the trenches and battlefields of World War One continued to be a daily ordeal, forever echoing in their minds to leave them wan, sickly ghosts.

"We shall soon be at Collinwood," William Collins said in his rasping voice. "I know you and your husband must be weary."

Aroused from her reverie, she told the older man, "It is harder for John than for me. His health is still in a delicate state."

"That seems obvious," William Collins agreed.

At once John looked angry. "I wish you wouldn't draw attention to me," he said accusingly. "It is bad enough to be as I am without being pointed at."

She touched his arm placatingly. "Please, John, I meant no harm. You aren't long out of the hospital yet, and the journey has been difficult for you."

"I'm not an invalid," he said firmly, "and I refuse to be treated as one."

They had rounded a bend in the road and now ahead of them on the right she saw a dark, sprawling mansion with lights at many of its windows. She spoke up in a mildly excited tone, "That must be Collinwood ahead!"

"It is," William Collins agreed without moving in his seat. "I hope you and John have a pleasant stay with us."

"I'm sure we shall," she said gratefully, not knowing how far from the truth that statement was destined to be!

CHAPTER 2

W illiam Collins and the housekeeper, a pleasant, middle-aged woman, saw Ann and John up to their rooms. Ann had requested that they have adjoining bedrooms, as he still seemed better in his own room and bed. She always left the door between the rooms open at night so as to be alert to any unusual sound which might signal the advent of another nightmare.

Their host had invited them to come down for a goodnight sherry and to meet his son when they were settled, and Ann waited until they were alone before asking John solicitously, "Do you feel well enough to go downstairs for a little?"

John Hayward's noble face was a mask of weariness as he looked down at her and pleaded, "You really mustn't try to make an invalid of me."

"I'm not. But I don't want you to overdo yourself," she worried.

He touched her gently and kissed her on the forehead. "I'm tired, but a few minutes conversation and a sherry can't possibly harm me."

"Very well," she said. "But if your headache begins let me know and we'll find an excuse to leave at once."

He smiled sadly. "Your only fault as a wife is that you can't get over being a nurse."

"That's hard to do when the man I love is both my husband and a patient."

"A former patient," he corrected her. "I was discharged from the hospital."

"In my care," she reminded him. "We must contact a doctor here at once. There are your prescriptions to be filled and you'll still need regular check-ups."

John sighed. "It seems I've always been on leave from the hospital… as if my life began with my being a patient."

She gave him an affectionate smile. "And I hoped you felt it began when you married me."

"That's also true," he agreed, his arm around her. "Let us go downstairs so I can show you off. My pretty wife!"

The living room of Collinwood was paneled in rich dark wood. Its walls were graced by framed portraits of members of the family and scenes of the shore and surrounding countryside. The furniture was heavy and magnificent. There was a great stone fireplace at one end of the big room, in front of which their host was standing with two younger men when Ann and John came to join them.

A reluctant smile crossed William Collins' bleak face as he greeted them. "Glad you weren't too tired to come down." He turned to a handsome blond youth with a devil-may-care air about him and said, "This is my son, Eric."

Ann shook hands with him. "I'm happy to meet you. My husband has spoken of you often."

"We're old friends," Eric Collins assured her warmly and turned to John, "Glad to have you back, John."

"Thank you," John said quietly.

William Collins now waved the other young man forward. "And just so you won't feel isolated here, this is a compatriot of yours, my cousin from England, Barnabas Collins."

Ann smiled at the good-looking man in the tweed suit who stood before her. "How nice to meet someone from home!"

"I'm glad to meet you, Mrs. Hayward," he said. As he took her hand, she was surprised by the coldness of his touch.

"Are you from London?" she asked. She was impressed by his strong, though somewhat gaunt face, his brownish hair with a stray lock carelessly across his broad forehead, the deep-set brown eyes that seemed to see through you.

"Yes. I have lived mostly in London," he said, gravely.

"What did you do in the war?" It was an almost automatic question to ask any Englishman. In the war just ended even the older men had been called into service.

"Because of a health problem I was not in the regular

army," he said quietly. "But I worked in a civilian post at General Headquarters."

Ann smiled as John joined them. "My husband was in the United States Army and we met while he was recovering from shell shock."

Barnabas held out a hand to John. "Of course I remember you," he said. "We met at least once when I paid a previous visit to the village."

"That is true. I think you were regarded as a man of mystery. You rarely came into the village during the days."

Barnabas smiled faintly. "Then I still must qualify as the mysterious stranger. I'm working on a family history and give all my days to it. Only in the evenings do I show myself."

"I think people should be entitled to keep whatever hours suit them," Ann defended him.

"I agree," Barnabas said with a bow. "But in a village when dawn to dusk are the hours of activity it is hard to make anyone understand."

William Collins brought Ann and John their sherries. John moved away with him to talk to Eric, leaving Ann and Barnabas alone. Not that she felt uneasy with the charming Englishman. In fact, she had been drawn to him at once.

When they were alone, he said, "I can see that your husband is still ill. There is a vast change in him since we last met. All these young men shattered this way is a sad commentary on the futility of war."

"I couldn't agree more," she assured him. "I will have to take good care of John. He is not yet as well as he thinks."

"We have another war casualty here in the village," Barnabas told her. "A young man who has rented a cottage down the beach. I've only passed him a few times and not really had any conversation with him, but I understand he was badly wounded in the battle of Chateau Thierry. Most of his face was shot away. Though he has had plastic surgery, the story goes that one side of his face was too badly damaged for repair. He wears a black silk mask to cover it, though the other side is bare. He also wears dark glasses so it is hard to tell what he really looks like."

She gave a tiny shudder. "I've seen similar cases."

"He lives the life of a recluse, so it is possible you may never encounter him. I just thought you might be interested."

"I am," she said. "You're not living here permanently, then?"

"No," Barnabas said. "I come every now and then for visits of various lengths. I stay at the old house—it's less than a mile from here."

"Then we'll see you frequently."

"I promise you that," he assured her. "Your new house appears to be coming along very well."

"I'm very interested in it," she said. "Is it a long way from Collinwood?"

"Not really," he said. "It's closer to the village on the main highway, but it should have a fine view of the bay from its upper stories."

"Collinwood is right on the water," she said.

"Yes. That gives it a special setting," Barnabas agreed, "though some people think it is too near the cliffs."

"I'm sure I'll like it," she said.

At that moment, Eric moved over to join them. With a mocking smile for Barnabas, he said, "You mustn't believe everything our British cousin tells you."

She smiled. "I'm sure he's very reliable."

"You're prejudiced because he's a fellow-countryman," Eric Collins said. "But for any important information you'd do well to rely on me."

Barnabas looked amused. "In that case I need have no compunctions about leaving her in your hands." He bowed to Ann. "Goodnight, Mrs. Hayward, I look forward to our next meeting. We can talk more about England."

She said goodnight to him and he went on to say his farewells to the other men, then left the room. Eric had taken up a stand by her and eyed his cousin's departure. Now he gave his full attention to her.

"What do you think of our Barnabas?" he asked.

"He seems a gentleman," she said.

"He has charm," Eric agreed, gesturing with the half-empty liquor glass in his hand. His fair skin was flushed from an evening of drinking. "But there are other things about him that may not be so pleasant."

She frowned. "I find that hard to believe."

"You'll see," he promised her and took a sip of his drink. "You'll learn a lot of things before you've been long in this house of ghosts and vampires."

His comment amazed her. "Aren't you giving Collinwood an evil reputation?"

He shrugged, "No more than it deserves."

"I've looked forward to my visit here," she said. "No one told me anything about the house having such a wicked reputation."

"Collinwood is a place of dark legends," Eric assured her, "a place of dark shadows."

"I hope I'm not bothered by any of them."

"So do I," Eric said. "But it only seemed fair to warn you as it seemed proper to give you a hint about Barnabas. Over the years stories have grown around Collinwood. It is the haunted house of the area, the place where phantoms are seen and a werewolf was once supposed to roam the grounds."

"That's fantastic!" she gasped.

"Yet the rumor became so strong that one of my ancestors, Quentin Collins, had to leave the estate. He was the one they thought had sold his soul to the devil."

"He never returned?"

"That's a story in itself," Eric said with another of those tormenting smiles. "There are rumors he has come back for visits— always disguised as someone else."

"Do you believe them?"

"I don't think so," the young man said. "At least there haven't been any werewolves around here lately. The vampire thing is something else."

"Vampires?" she asked in surprise.

He nodded. "The living dead who survive by feasting on the blood of the living. You must have heard of them. I think everyone has at least read the novel *Dracula*. At Collinwood, we've been said to have our own version of Dracula."

"It sounds utterly fantastic," she said.

"Ask Barnabas to tell you more about it," Eric suggested with a twinkle in his eyes. "He knows all the Collinwood legends, since he collects them for his history."

"I had no idea my husband and I were visiting such an exciting place," Ann said.

He studied her in the soft, mellow light and glanced in the direction of John and his father. When he was sure they weren't listening, he said in a low voice, "John is some wreck, isn't he?"

Her cheeks burned at this crude comment about her husband. "He's still suffering from his war injuries," she said pointedly to this young man who clearly had not been in the services.

"I wonder that an attractive girl like you would tie yourself to him," Eric went on, seemingly unaware that she resented his tone.

"I love John," was her quiet reply.

"Don't think I'm not wishing you good luck," the blond youth said hastily. "But I doubt whether such a marriage can be fair to you."

"We've known a lot of happiness thus far," Ann insisted, annoyed at the young man and wishing she could escape talking to him.

"And you've dared the Hayward curse in coming back here," Eric taunted her.

She frowned. "The Hayward curse?"

"Surely he told you about it?" Eric said with a show of surprise, but whether it was feigned or real she couldn't decide.

"I've never heard anything about it," Ann said. "Are you baiting me with some story?"

"I wouldn't think of it," he protested. "The legend of the Hayward brides goes back a century or more to the days when Collinsport was a lot smaller than it is at present. People in villages were really isolated then."

"So?"

"So they rarely married outside their immediate areas. Once in a long while someone would journey back to the town where he was born or visit one of the big cities and find himself a bride. But it happened infrequently. Most of the brides were chosen from among the other families in the village."

She smiled thinly. "And husbands as well, I trust."

"Correct," he said. "But the Haywards were never satisfied with village girls. Most of them found their brides in some distant places and brought them back here."

"Then John is merely carrying on the tradition."

"No argument there," Eric said. "But he is also defying the curse. There is a legend that every bride brought back by a Hayward met a tragic death, and it seems that history bears out that it happened that way. So strong was the superstition I've heard John's father and grandfather both publicly state they would go no further than the village for their wives. And they didn't. But now John has gone back to the old ways."

Ann listened to this with growing uneasiness and disbelief. She said, "I'm sure John isn't a type to be influenced by silly superstitions. That is why he married me and told me nothing about this so-called curse."

"That's probably the story," Eric agreed mockingly. "I hope you don't hold anything against me for mentioning it."

She gave him a very direct look. "I don't think you picked the best time for your revelations. My husband and I are very tired."

"Sorry," he said, but he didn't sound it. "I admire you so much that I want to offer you every protection. It seemed right you should be aware of the legend."

"You hardly know me," she said.

"I've known you long enough to decide what type of person you are," he said. "I think John is lucky... maybe luckier than he deserves."

She resented this much too pointed remark and turned her back on Eric and rejoined his father and John.

William Collins said, "Well, you've met both Barnabas and my son."

"Yes," she replied quietly.

"Barnabas is something of an eccentric," the crotchety elder Collins said, "but he is a brilliant man."

"I like him," she told William Collins.

"You would understand him since you are both English," he replied. "I trust you will like Collinsport."

"I'm sure she will," John said in a weary voice. "It is a friendly village and a pleasant area."

"I met so many Americans in the hospitals I feel I understand this country better than many English people might," Ann volunteered.

William Collins looked bleak. "I was not one of those who favored our entry into the war, and I surely think we should remain outside the League of Nations. We should not get ourselves mixed up in European politics."

"But surely, sir, the League is our best hope for world peace," John said.

William Collins frowned. "I am one of those who think first of the interests of America rather than the world. We have an ocean on either side of us to give us protection from Europe and Asia."

John accepted this reproof grimly. "I consider that a dangerous way of thinking, sir. Airplanes played a large part in the war. If we have another war they probably will be the deciding factor. I don't think it will be too long before you see planes crossing the Atlantic, either."

Eric Collins, who had joined their group, now sneered at John, saying, "That's sheer nonsense!"

"Wait and see," her husband said quietly. He turned to her, "I have a headache. I think I should go upstairs."

"Of course," she said. "Please excuse us," she asked the other two men. Goodnights were said all around and she and John mounted the shadowed stairway to their rooms.

When they were safely inside the privacy of their rooms, John said worriedly. "We may have made a mistake in coming here. We don't seem to see eye to eye with William Collins or his son."

"I don't mind the old man," she said. "He is getting along in years and bound to be set in his views. But I dislike Eric."

"He always had a nasty disposition and a quick temper. His brother, Tom, was a much nicer person."

"That's not hard to believe," she said, studying him closely. "Are you all right?"

"I think so," he said. "My head did start to pound and I felt I'd better get away from them."

"You did right," she declared. She wanted to ask him about the curse of the Hayward brides but realized this would be the wrong time. She'd have to wait and bring this up again. "You'd better go to bed at once," she advised.

"Yes, you're right," he agreed. "It has been a long day and night."

She saw him safely in bed and then returned to her own bedroom, leaving the door open between them. Collinwood had not yet been wired for electricity and the rooms were lit by ornate lamps and candles. A good-sized lamp, with a fancy enamel base decorated with flowers and brass, sat on her bedside table. She'd extinguished the lamp in John's room and now she turned down the wick of this one and blew the flame out.

Slipping between the cool sheets of her bed, she stared up at the velvet canopy above her in the darkness. Her mind went back to her conversation with Eric. He had done a good job of frightening her. His talk of werewolves, ghosts and vampires had been upsetting enough, but when he'd also brought up the legend of the Hayward brides, he'd really worried her.

He'd strongly hinted that she was a candidate for this unhappy fate. She couldn't understand why John hadn't told her about the legend. At least he could have presented it to her as an amusing fable and they might have laughed about it. The fact he'd kept silent had the unhappy effect of suggesting that he might believe in it. Perhaps he'd kept quiet about it for fear of losing her. Now that he'd brought her back to Collinsport, she would have to take her chances.

It was alarming and she made up her mind to query Barnabas about it. She felt sure she'd found a friend in the Collins' English cousin. It struck her that he was someone she could turn to if things really became rough. And she knew only too well that they could.

John had by no means fully recovered from his shell shocked state. He was one of the many examples of human wreckage left after a war. The man who had rented the cottage on the beach must be another. She felt a wave of sympathy for the unknown man Barnabas had described whose ravaged face had made him a recluse. She knew how gruesome such mutilation could be since she'd worked beside surgeons in field operating tents.

The elder Collins had angered her with his cold remarks about Europe and the war. Such Americans hardly realized the ordeal her native England had gone through to help defend a Europe which was isolated from them by the English channel. They did not understand the times into which the world was moving. John had attempted to give the Collinses some ideas but they had coldly rejected them.

Ann was ready to agree that planning a long stay at Collinwood could be considered a mistake. She'd been ready to admit this to her husband just now but had not wanted to upset him further. It would be best to wait until he was rested a little before she suggested making other arrangements. But she would do this at the first likely opportunity.

Ann strained to hear if John had gone to sleep, but there was no sound of heavy breathing from the adjoining room. She hoped he would be able to rest and not have one of those awful nights. When the bad spells came she had to give him strong sedatives which did not always take effect immediately.

She couldn't stop herself from thinking of what Eric Collins had said about the Hayward brides. It had to be sheer nonsense. She did not believe in such legends. No doubt several wives of Haywards had been unfortunate enough to suffer violent deaths and this had started the story. You had to close your mind to such things. John would never have deliberately placed her in such danger. He must consider the legend a ridiculous fable. She resolved to talk to Barnabas about it.

This decision reached, Ann felt a little less uneasy. She closed her eyes, realizing how dreadfully tired she was. The regular wash of the waves on the distant shore came to her with a hypnotic effect and she soon slipped into a sound sleep. Yet it was a sleep in which strange dreams played a part.

She dreamt she was walking along a rocky beach. Cliffs ranged up on the shore side shutting her off from any houses or people. She was quite alone. The waves came in with an angry rush and show of foam on the wet sands near where she walked. The ocean was vast and empty. She continued her lonely stroll filled with a sense of apprehension.

A lone figure was coming towards her. She halted and was about to retreat towards the cliffs and the path that would lead to safety above. But she had waited too long and soon the tall, dark-clad figure was within twenty feet of her. She was able to see him clearly.

She stared at his face in horror.

It was a face just as Eric had described to her. One side was neatly covered by a black silk bandage. And this stranger also wore dark glasses. He came directly towards her but she could neither run nor scream. She was paralyzed by a strange fear. His hands reached out for her and she began to sob in terror.

She opened her eyes with a start and sat up in the darkness. The dream was still vivid but now she realized it had been a dream inspired by the eerie story of the war-mutilated stranger which Eric had told her. She pressed a hand over her rapidly beating heart and stared around her in the darkness.

Only then was the terror of her dream replaced by fresh fear of the darkness surrounding her. She had a strong sense that she was not alone. There was someone lurking in the shadows close to her bed—someone who presented a menace to her.

And then she guessed who it was. The wearying day and night had been too much for the shattered nervous system of her husband. John had been seized by one of his spells of near madness. Undoubtedly, he was standing there in the darkness, in a sleepwalking state, staring at her.

She spoke his name, "John!"

There was no reply. The dark room was ominously silent as she waited for an answer. All the time her fear was building. She was recalling those other occasions when he'd been overcome by the delirium that occasionally haunted him.

In a tremulous voice she called out to him again. "John!"

The sound of her voice faded into the silence of the dark room. And then she thought she saw a hint of motion close by the side of her bed and she quickly moved away to the other side, straining to see some sign of movement again.

Swallowing hard, she said, "John, if that is you, please answer me!"

But there was no answer. She had begun to lose hope that there would be. Now she began to worry that it wasn't John who threatened her from the shadows, but some unknown menace, possibly one of the ghosts Eric had mockingly claimed the old house was host to. Was she being visited by some phantom of a long-dead Collins?

Or perhaps a vampire! Eric had fairly gloated over that legend. He had built up her fears for this moment. As she waited there, trembling, she distinctly heard a floorboard squeak. It was close by the bed. And with a swift movement she swung her feet over the other side of the bed and stood on the cool floor. She waited apprehensively.

Again she felt it had to be her sick husband. These other fears of ghosts were too ridiculous!

Making a final attempt to bring a response from the tormented mate who stood there somewhere in the dark, she cried out, "John! Please! Say something!"

Of course he didn't answer. Now she began to stealthily move down the length of the big bedroom. She was attempting a maneuver to reach the door leading to the hallway. If she made it safely she could summon help to assist her with a demented John or whatever other threat lingered there in the darkness.

She moved a single step at a time. But it was a long, nerve-wracking business. Every second that passed convinced her more there was a presence stalking her from the other side of the room. If she made one revealing sound she was certain she would at once be attacked. Hardly daring to breathe she managed to edge closer to the door that would lead to safety.

In the darkness it was hard to tell how well she was doing. By her own calculations she couldn't be more than five or six feet from that important door.

Then disaster overtook her with sickening swiftness. She stumbled against a chair which was in her path. And with that sound another quickly followed—from across the room she heard and felt the advance of that sinister intruder.

"John!" she again called out in panic.

Then the stalking figure was upon her and cruel, strong hands grasped her. She launched out with her fists and hit at her unseen assailant. For just a second she escaped. With a scream of terror she raced across the room in the darkness, hoping to reach John's room and close the door between her and this mad phantom.

But she'd barely gone a couple of steps before the fierce hands reached out to grasp her once more. She cried out and tried to fight free of this sinister thing once again, but without any success. Now she felt his hot breath on her face and heard his hoarse irregular breathing. She identified these things with John's earlier seizures. She felt sure it was her unfortunate, shell-shocked husband who was attempting to strangle her.

"John, it's Ann! Please let me go!" she begged as his hands closed on her throat in a crazy grip. Her breath was gradually being shut off and she was slipping into unconsciousness. Her last thought was that the legend might have some truth in it after all and another Hayward bride from the outside was about to die violently!

CHAPTER 3

A nn opened her eyes and looked up to see John standing above her. His emaciated face wore a blank expression and he held a candleholder with a lighted candle in his hand. The candle's glow showed his dazed face clearly though the rest of the room was still shadowed in darkness. Remembrance came back to her quickly. Her throat pained and her head ached as she recalled being pursued from the other room by a phantom figure.

Staring up at John's stunned face, she knew he must have been her attacker. He'd luckily recovered from his delirium and let her go, and now he was confused and worried about her, not remembering what had happened. This was how it had been those other times.

The dull eyes stared down at her. "Ann, what is it?" he asked, bewildered.

She raised herself on an elbow. "Nothing for you to worry about."

"But I am worried," he protested. "What happened?"

Ann didn't want to upset him more than he was. Shakily, she got to her feet. "Someone tried to attack me," she said. "Didn't you hear anything?"

The candle's glow illuminated his head and shoulders. Terror showed in his eyes. "I can't remember anything," he confessed, trembling. "It's all a blank."

She touched his arm reassuringly. "Don't worry about it."

"But I must," he insisted. "Did I have another nightmare? Am I the one who attacked you?"

Ann fully believed he had been responsible, but she had no wish to hurl guilt at her unfortunate husband. She knew his madness could not be controlled when the spells of fury came to him.

Truthfully, she said, "I have no idea whether it was you or a stranger. In any case, it's over and I'm all right. You're trembling dreadfully. You must get back to bed."

John obeyed her quietly, with the same resignation as if he were still a patient at the hospital. When the delirium left him he was always meek and repentant. She felt a deep pity for the state this fine young man had been left in by the war. She stood by until he had slipped between the sheets and then straightened the bed.

He was staring at her piteously. "I'm afraid we made a bad mistake in coming to this house," he worried.

"Why?"

"Collinwood is not a lucky place," he said, "and William Collins and his son are difficult. I have the feeling they resent us even though they did invite us here as their guests."

"I'm sure we can get along with them," she said.

"I hope so," he sighed.

Ann managed a smile that was hard to summon, but she knew he had to be put as much at ease as possible. "Now do try to sleep," she said.

"I think I will," he told her hollowly. "I'm very weary."

"That is good," she said. She knew this was the pattern. After one of his spells he was left in an exhausted state. He would likely sink into a deep sleep. It would be some time before he awakened.

She watched as he closed his eyes and then extinguished the candle and went back to her own bed. It had been a narrow escape for her, but it had not been entirely unexpected since she'd known that John had been overtired and his spells and blackouts usually followed exhaustion. She pulled the covers around her and worried that some of the noise from their rooms might have drifted to the rest of the house. But she consoled herself with the thought that Collinwood was a very large place and their rooms were fairly well isolated. The fact that no one had come to enquire what was happening was also a sign they hadn't been heard by the others.

She finally managed to sleep. Morning came and it was warm and sunny. John awoke in a more rested mood and with apparently no memory of what had happened the night before. Ann made no mention of it and they went down to join the others at breakfast.

The elder Collins was at the table. He rose with napkin in

hand as they came in and waved them to chairs. "My son, Eric, usually has his breakfast in his room," William Collins explained in his precise way. "He is not associated with the family business at the present and so his time is mostly his own, though he is raising and supervising the training of some fine horses."

Ann smiled at him. "On a day like this you really appreciate the lovely setting of Collinwood."

"Very true," William Collins said. "I trust the fresh air and warm weather and sunshine will help your recovery, John."

John's sallow, thin face lighted up as he said, "Thank you, I'm sure it will. At the moment, I'm extremely anxious to see how the workmen are getting along with our new home."

"I'll see that a carriage is placed at your disposal," Collins promised. "Then you can take a drive over there this morning."

He proved as good as his word. By the time they had finished breakfast, the carriage was waiting by the front entrance.

Ann, sitting beside him on the driver's seat, was pleased to see the glow of pleasure on his face as he took the reins. "You seem very much at home with horses," she said.

"I am," he said, glancing at her with an eager smile. "I had my own pair of chestnut stallions and a fine carriage before I joined the army."

"You'll have them again," she promised.

"I hope so," he answered.

As they drove along the narrow country road in the sunshine, none of what had happened last night seemed so bad. When John's spells passed, Ann always fastened her hopes on the chance there would be no others. But this was playing herself false for she had been warned by all the doctors at the hospital that he was an almost incurable case.

The morning they had left the hospital the eminent gray haired doctor had taken her aside. "I hope you know what you are doing, young woman," he said sternly. "This is a very sick man you are planning to marry."

She'd given the physician an imploring look and said, "Surely he is bound to improve as time goes on. He is young, and was in fine health until he received his war injuries."

"We don't know too much about shell shock yet," the physician admitted. "But what we do know, we don't like. I shouldn't have to tell you how many wards of our hospitals contain shell-shocked veterans, seemingly in a hopeless state. John Hayward's condition is not that acute—but it is serious."

"I still intend to marry him," she said solemnly.

"That must be your own decision," the doctor sighed. "But I make no promises... and I urge you to take care. You are dealing with someone who has suffered mental damage."

All that had taken place months ago. Now, here she was in a new world on her way to see the home John was having built for her. She had to believe he would improve. One day they would be able to enjoy the normal, happy lives of other married people.

They reached the main highway and drove for a half-mile. Then, ahead on the right, she saw that the foundation had been laid and the walls were already being erected at the site of her new home. The builders were hard at work.

She gave John an excited glance. "It's a fine location. Almost as good as Collinwood, though it is not as near the ocean."

John looked pleased. "I'm glad you approve. We're using the foundation of the original house. It wasn't damaged too badly in the fire."

It took them a few minutes more to reach the rising structure. John tied up the horses and helped her from the carriage. They strolled across to the bustling scene and were greeted by the elderly foreman.

He touched his hand to his cap and with a friendly smile said, "Good to see you back, Mr. Hayward. And this will be your missus, I expect."

"That's right, Sam," John said, staring at the construction. Seeming like his old self, he introduced them. "Sam is the best builder in the area," he assured her.

Sam accepted the compliment with pleasure. He took them over to the building and pointed out where the various rooms would be. He gave a date, two months ahead, as the earliest possible time they could move in.

"I hear you are living at Collinwood now," he said, a veiled look on his weathered face.

"Yes, we are," she agreed.

"Do you like it?" the builder asked.

She smiled embarrassedly. "We've only just arrived. Mr. Collins and his son seem very nice."

"Old Will is a good enough man," the builder said, "but I wouldn't put too much stock in what that Eric says. He spends most of his time drinking and betting on the races. He owns two or three race horses himself."

"So we understand," John said.

"Still, that's not my business," Sam sighed. "But I'd mind myself at Collinwood. It's one of those old places loaded with secret passages and plenty of ghosts to fill them!"

Ann listened to this startling statement with some surprise. "Does that mean all the stories you hear about it are true?"

The builder shrugged. "I have heard workmen who've done

repairs there tell of secret passages which lead from floor to floor. From basement to attic there are hidden steps and corridors. That's a queer house."

John gave him a reproving glance. "If you keep on that way, my wife will be too nervous to remain there."

"Sorry," Sam said, "just felt she should know the kind of place it is. And then there's that fellow Barnabas. I hear he's back again."

Ann stared at him. "But I find Barnabas charming!"

"Maybe you don't know him as well as some," the old man said bleakly, but offered no explanation of this as he went on showing them the building and telling what he planned to do. It was an hour before they got away.

They drove the rest of the short distance to the steep main street of Collinsport village, down as far as the wharf where the nightboat from Boston still arrived at midnight, three times a week.

Ann was delighted with the quaint village. Its weatherbeaten one-story shops thrilled her. John pointed out the hardware store and the Blue Whale Tavern across the street from it. Further up the street they came to the hotel, a three-story building painted a dingy white, and the post office. He showed her the side street where the doctor's office was located. All in all, it gave her a fine idea of the place.

Then they took the winding road back to Collinwood. John drove slowly and seemed thoughtful. "Did you like the house?" he asked.

"I think it will be perfect for us," she said.

A shadow came across his thin face as he told her, "Somehow I can't ever picture its being completed or our ever living in it."

His tone was so desolate that a chill of fear shot through her. "Why do you say that?"

"I can't explain it," he admitted, holding the reins loosely in his hands as the horses jogged along. "It's just a feeling I have."

"You mustn't have such somber thoughts," she told him.

"I suppose not," he sighed. "But I can't forget how sick I still am. You know that better than anyone else."

"And I know you'll get better," she comforted.

"No fault on your part if I don't," he said with a warm smile. "The best thing that ever happened was when you agreed to marry me."

"It was fine for me," she said.

"You knew I'd never likely come back to complete health," John said, "and yet you were willing to share the future with me."

"And it will be a fine future," she said. Under the warm sun, it was easy for her to push aside her fears.

"I feel I'm not being fair to you," John worried as they came within sight of Collinwood.

It seemed an ideal moment to ask about the superstition which had been troubling her. "What is this legend I hear about the Hayward brides? That any wife of a Hayward from outside the village is doomed to die in some tragic fashion? Surely you should have told me about that!"

Her husband gave her an anxious glance. "Where did you hear that story?"

"Didn't you want me to hear it?"

"Who told you about it?"

"Eric. Last night."

"I might have known," John said grimly. "It would take someone like him to do a thing like that!"

She smiled. "Of course I know it's merely a legend. But how did it ever get its start?"

He was frowning. "Three Hayward brides—all from outside the area—died violently in a century and a half. That was all it took to get the story going."

"I wondered why you hadn't told me."

"Because it is obviously nonsense," he said angrily. "Eric only mentioned it to cause trouble!"

"But I felt I should tell you what he said," she added quickly.

"You were right in that," he said, somewhat placated. "We should have no secrets from each other. If this worried you I agree you have done right in mentioning it. But I can assure you it's merely a legend repeated by the ignorant and should have no concern for us."

She sat close to him. "Of course I realize that," she agreed. "I only told you to get it off my mind."

"Watch out for that Eric," John warned her. "I've known him since he was a boy. He is headstrong and selfish... I could tell he's got an eye on you. That's why he is anxious to cause trouble between us by repeating that silly legend."

"It's done with," she said soothingly. "I'll think no more about it. We must try to fit in at Collinwood if we're to remain for a month or two."

They had reached the great mansion and John helped her down from the carriage. "I'll take the rig back to the stables," he said. "Then I'll have a nap before dinner. The drive has tired me."

"Do that," she said, anxious to encourage him to take all the rest he could.

"What about you?"

"I'll manage nicely," she said. "I'm going to stroll along the cliffs. The view is magnificent."

"Be careful," he warned her. "The path goes near the edge of the cliffs and the drop is sheer."

"I'll be cautious," she promised.

She'd not gone far along the path when she came to a junction with another path that led down a sloping section of the cliffs, to the shore below. The idea of walking near the ocean intrigued her into taking the downward path. It was precariously steep and uneven, but she reached the rocky beach without mishap.

Ann was strolling along the wet sand for a few minutes when she began to have the feeling that she had been there before. She halted, staring first at the cliffs towering above her on one side, and the ocean stretching out on the other. It was obviously impossible— she'd never been on the beach before—and yet it seemed familiar!

All at once she knew the explanation. Her dream! In her dream she had strolled on a beach like this. It all came back to her in a rush. She remembered that as the dream had progressed she'd met a man walking towards her—a man who resembled the one Barnabas had described. He'd worn a black bandage to hide one side of his mutilated face, and black glasses. The details of it all sent a nervous thrill through her.

She resumed her walking, astonished at how much the reality resembled her dream. It was hard to believe, almost as if she'd experienced second sight.

Ann stopped close to the wash of the waves, lost in a reverie of all that had taken place since her arrival at Collinwood. Suddenly, she had a feeling of danger, of being watched by someone.

Staring ahead, she saw a thin, dark-clad male figure a hundred yards or so distant along the beach, standing alone, with his gaze obviously fixed on her—just as it had happened in her dream!

Panic seized her and she felt a strong desire to avoid a meeting with this stranger. She was sure he was the mutilated war victim whom Barnabas had described as a rather sinister figure. Now they were down here alone, isolated from the rest of Collinwood.

The feeling of fear grew in her. She was certain that malevolent eyes were focused on her. On a sudden impulse, she turned from the sandy stretch of the beach and rushed to the bottom of the cliffs in search of a hiding place among the huge boulders there. She found a high one that would successfully screen her from the beach, where she might hide until the stranger had passed. She pressed herself between the rock and the base of the cliff.

Ann had barely concealed herself there, keeping her anxious eyes on the stranger as he moved closer, when there was another, unexpected, happening. From above, a shower of rocks and earth rained down around her. She cried out in terror and dashed out of her hiding place— and was confronted by the stranger.

He was the figure of her dream.

He might have been handsome, but for the black silk covering one half of his face and his dark glasses. He was well-dressed, and his dark suit and soft hat of the same dark shade showed taste.

Now he doffed his hat, revealing thick, curly black hair, and said, "That was a nasty landslide. Are you hurt?"

Her shoulders and the front of her dress still had some earth on them. Ann was blushing as she brushed herself off and told him, "Luckily, I escaped most of the rocks."

He looked up at the cliff. "I saw you dart towards the cliff before it happened, and I was sure I saw someone up there. They may have walked too close to the edge and started the landslide."

"It came very near to me."

"An odd coincidence," the man said, studying her. Something in his tone hinted that he did not consider it a coincidence at all, but a planned happening.

Ann was frightened and embarrassed. Her ploy to escape a meeting with the scarred young man had ended in disaster. She began to suspect that her feeling of danger and eyes upon her had come from another source. Perhaps the malevolence had been directed at her from someone high on the cliffs above—someone who had waited for a chance to harm her and had almost managed it.

She gave a tiny shudder. "Any one of those larger rocks could have caved in my skull if it had struck me directly."

"I'm afraid so," the man said gravely. "In the future I'd keep away from the bottom of those cliffs."

"I will," she promised.

The dark glasses seemed to study her. "May I introduce myself?" the young man said in his pleasant voice. "My name is Warren Miller. I have rented a cottage further along the shore."

"I'm Ann Hayward," she said. "My husband and I are guests at Collinwood while our new home is being built."

"Of course," he said. "You're the English nurse who cared for John in the hospital and married him."

She looked at him in surprise. "You seem to know all about us!"

"Collinsport is a small place," he apologized. "I have some friends here who retail the local gossip to me, though I'm not acquainted with William Collins or his son."

"You've been to the village before?"

"Yes. I've come here over the years," he said, a hint of sadness in his tone. "But this is my first visit since the war."

"You've probably heard that my husband suffers from shell

shock," she said.

"Yes," Warren Miller answered. "Has he made a good recovery?"

"I feel he is improving all the time."

"I'm glad to hear that," the tall, slender man said sympathetically. "I also suffered injuries in the army. As you can see, they are too obvious to need explaining."

She felt sorry for him. "They are doing marvels with plastic surgery these days."

"So I've been assured," he said with bitterness. "One side of my face was restored. The other proved too difficult. I'm to report to the hospital again in a few months. Until then, I'm trying to keep to myself."

Ann frowned. "Is that necessary?"

"I feel so."

"Wouldn't you be better working at whatever it was you did?"

"I was an actor," Warren Miller said grimly, "and there are few parts available for leading men wearing silk masks over half their faces."

"I'm sorry," she apologized.

"Quite all right," he said. "How could you know? And incidentally, I like your accent."

"Thank you," she said. "I was so sure people would find it odd over here."

"Not at all," he said. "I think most Americans admire the pure British accent."

"Barnabas Collins has one," she told him.

The half-face that was revealed showed a smile. "You have met Barnabas?"

"Last night."

"Of course. He'd be at Collinwood then."

"You know him?"

"By reputation," he said carefully. "If you like, I'll walk along with you as far as the path leading up the cliff."

"Thank you," she said, gratefully accepting the invitation.

"It is suitably isolated for me here," the man at her side said as they walked. "And I amuse myself by reading and having some of the juicier scandals of the area repeated to me."

She smiled. "I'm sure there are plenty of them."

He nodded. "The people—and even the big house—at Collinwood supply many of the bits of gossip. Eric Collins is a suitably dissolute young man. His misbehavior has kept him on people's tongues."

Ann had no doubt Warren Miller was telling the truth about

Eric, but she had no wish to offer an opinion, being new to the estate. She said, "I've only talked with him briefly."

"That should be enough to tell you about him," Warren assured. "And Collinwood is rumored to be a haunted mansion. They even speak of vampires and werewolves in conjunction with it."

She gave him a rueful smile. "My imagination doesn't stretch that far."

"It might before you leave Collinwood," he told her pointedly.

"I hope not."

"So do I," he said, casting a meaningful glance her way, "but you can never tell about these things. You should talk to Barnabas Collins. He can tell you more than most people. He's the historian of the family."

"I understand that."

"Ask him about Quentin Collins," the man with the mask said. "And when we meet again, tell me what he has to say about him."

"Quentin Collins interests you?"

"Yes. I think he fascinates many people. Some years ago he left here under a dark shadow, after he had been accused of being a werewolf."

"You can't believe that he was?" she asked in surprise.

He shrugged. "I try to keep an open mind, but I had a passing acquaintance with him and I don't consider him the villain he has been depicted as."

"I doubt that he is," Ann was quick to agree. "In fact, I question the existence of werewolves."

Warren glanced at her sharply. "You may have a good point there," he said. "But in this sleepy little village remote from the real world, people still get their thrills from such superstitious tales."

"It's hard to imagine in this day and age," she said.

"I agree," Warren said. "I suppose that is why Collinsport fascinates me... why I keep returning. It has been untouched by the events of our time."

They had reached the foot of the path and Ann stopped to thank him for his company. "I'm grateful to you for seeing me safely here."

The uncovered side of his face showed a friendly look. "I've enjoyed talking to you. I trust we'll meet again under less exciting conditions."

"So do I."

"I walk every day," he said.

"You should come and visit at Collinwood," she suggested.

"I'm sure you'd be welcome."

He shook his head. "I draw the line there. I have some misgivings about that house and the people in it. I'm afraid they might look upon me as a freak and I wouldn't really be welcome."

Ann stared at him earnestly. "You shouldn't feel embarrassed about your face. Once one gets used to that black bandage, you're very presentable. I'm sure you were handsome before and I hope you will be again one day."

"That depends on the army doctors," the young man said solemnly. "But thank you for your kind words. They are comforting."

They parted and she walked up the steep path to the cliff. As she neared the top, she looked and saw that Warren had vanished. She was really glad she had met him.

Ann reached the level of the cliffs and walked along the path leading back to Collinwood. She'd only gone a short distance when she heard the sound of hoofbeats behind her. Turning quickly, she saw Eric come riding up on a spirited black horse.

He reined it to a nervous halt and smiled down at her. "I saw you on the beach."

"Oh?"

"You've lost no time meeting our mysterious stranger," Eric said with a mocking smile. "Were you impressed?"

"He's interesting," she said.

He held tightly on the reins of the veering black horse. "I have no doubt of that," he said. "We must discuss him later." With a parting nod and smile, he rode off.

Ann stared after him with puzzled eyes. Warren Miller had said he'd seen someone on the cliffs above her before that dangerous shower of earth and rocks had rained down, either accidentally or by devious plan. Could Eric have been the one whose malevolent eyes Ann had felt upon her?

CHAPTER 4

John complained of a headache after lunch, and returned to his room again. Ann decided this was an ideal opportunity to visit the old house on the estate and have a talk with Barnabas. She'd wanted to do this since her brief meeting with him the previous night. Now she finally had the chance.

She left Collinwood and followed the path that led past the stables and other outbuildings till she reached the red brick house. The drab shutters were closed and to all appearances, the house was deserted, but she knocked anyway.

After a long while, she heard shuffling footsteps inside and the door was opened just wide enough to reveal a broad, ugly face covered by a stubble of gray beard.

She said, "I've come to see Barnabas Collins."

In answer, the unkempt creature shook his head vigorously and made a low growling sound. And then, without further hesitation, the door was slammed closed in her face.

Ann felt hurt and frustrated. She was sure Barnabas wouldn't approve of this rude treatment. And yet, the person who had answered the door must be an employee of his, though a strange one, indeed.

She debated knocking again and then decided against it. She had no idea whether Barnabas was in the house or not. She might only annoy the odd servant further and suffer another brusque rebuff.

All she could do was wait to see Barnabas when he came to the main house later. She had an idea he made his visits during the evening.

She stood on the steps for a moment and surveyed the rolling field to the left that sloped down to a private burial ground, near the edge of a forest of evergreens. That would undoubtedly be the Collins family cemetery. She left the steps and started walking back in the direction of Collinwood.

On the way, she met William Collins. The elderly squire of the estate had apparently returned early from his office at the fish packing plant and was enjoying a brisk stroll around the grounds.

His stern face showed interest as he greeted her. "Finding your way around?"

"Yes," she said. "I wanted to talk to Barnabas. I went to the old house but a very strange servant answered the door and wouldn't let me in."

A grim smile crossed his face. "That was Hare. He travels constantly with Barnabas. He is devoted, but very eccentric. And, of course, he is a mute."

"That explains why he behaved so oddly," she said. "He made a sort of growling sound when I questioned him about Barnabas."

"All he can manage, poor fellow," William Collins said. "But he is remarkably intelligent and takes good care of Barnabas. My cousin works in a cellar study during the daytime and has issued strict orders he is never to be disturbed. That is why Hare closed the door to you."

"I didn't understand," she said. "I'm sorry I bothered him."

"No harm done," her host said. "You couldn't be expected to know." He paused rather awkwardly before he cleared his throat and added, "There is one other thing."

"Yes?"

"About Barnabas."

"Please go on," she said, puzzled by his sudden uneasiness.

"I have no idea why you wished to see him just now," he said, "but I feel I should warn you against him."

Her eyebrows raised. "Warn me?"

William Collins was having a hard time finding words to express himself. At last he said, "My British cousin has a certain charm. But our experience has been that he is not to be trusted."

"Why do you say that?"

"He has made previous visits here and several times there have been incidents concerning young women. Statements were made that he rather cruelly attacked several attractive village girls. I had to ask him to leave on two occasions when the ire of the village people had been aroused to the point of danger."

Ann stared at him. "I can't see Barnabas doing anything like that. He is an English gentleman."

"You are probably right," William Collins admitted. "The accusations against the present Barnabas Collins are probably not well-founded. He may even be completely innocent. However, the suspicion directed against him goes back more than a hundred years."

"I don't understand," she said.

"When you return to Collinwood take a moment to study a portrait in the lower hallway. It is a fine painting of the first Barnabas Collins. I'll vow that you'll think he bears a startling resemblance to the present holder of the name. The first Barnabas Collins was reputed to have been changed into a vampire by the bite of an infected bat. The bat was in the hands of a jealous woman who, because of her frustrated love, doomed that Barnabas Collins and his descendants to roam the world as members of the fraternity of the living dead."

"You're saying this Barnabas is also tainted by the same curse?"

"No. But I believe local gossips associate him with the sins of those who came before him."

"That is surely unfair."

"Still, that is the situation," the old man said firmly. "So my advice is to go slow in forming any close friendship with him."

Ann was angry that he should so presume to tell her whom she might choose as a friend. In a carefully controlled voice, she said, "I suppose because I'm English, I naturally have an inclination to turn towards your cousin. I find him understanding."

"I can see your position," William Collins said rather icily. "But let me remind you that the English branch of the Collins family was founded when that first Barnabas left here under suspicion of being a vampire. The shadow has hung over them all, down through the years."

"I still feel I can depend on this present Barnabas as a friend," she insisted quietly.

He looked displeased. "You are free to disregard my warning if you wish. I have done all I think is required of me. I have explained the situation."

"Thank you," she said.

"It will do you no good to try and contact Barnabas until after dusk," he added. "He often visits us at the main house in the early evening."

She gave him a sharp glance. "Is he aware of how you feel about him?"

"I assume so, since the matter has been brought into the open on his other visits. We are carrying on under a kind of truce, at present. If there should be any complaints from the village, I'd consider the gentleman's agreement broken and request Barnabas to leave at once. While there are no incidents, there shall be no trouble."

"Thanks for explaining it so fully," she said.

"You are my guest. I must attempt to protect you," Collins said with a brusque nod and walked on.

Ann continued towards the mansion. The story that William Collins had just told her seemed preposterous. It was unbelievable that the local people should be so backward as to still believe in vampires and werewolves! It was like the dark ages.

Ann was loath to enter the old mansion. Instead, she walked around to the rose garden at the left of the house and sat down on a wooden bench. Relaxing in the shadowed spot, she thought over all that she learned so far on this first day at Collinwood. She was beginning to understand why it was regarded as a house of phantoms!

Her mind was eased by the knowledge that John was resting a good deal. It was worth going through some unpleasant experiences to have him benefit from the quiet, restful atmosphere. She was sure things would be much better for them when they had their own home. Perhaps, by then, John would have improved in health to the point where his recurrent nightmare attacks would return no more. She counted on this against all the dire predictions of his doctors.

It was while these thoughts were going through her mind, that she once again experienced that chill sensation of being watched by eyes filled with hatred. It was as real as if a cold hand had reached out to touch her. She glanced up at the windows and quickly scanned the dark squares, finding them all empty...

All empty until she reached a window on the third floor and saw a white, hate-twisted face staring down at her. She uttered a tiny cry of alarm for it was Eric Collins who was studying her with such sneering hatred. She couldn't understand why he should feel this way about her. She looked up again and the curtain flicked back in place, and the face vanished.

Ann sat there in consternation. Eric had been described as a dissolute character, but never as mad, yet he was showing a weird pattern of behavior. Had he another personality, one which most people were unaware of? It seemed so. Persons of that type had crafty ways of concealing their true natures.

The pleasant atmosphere of the garden had been ruined and the memory of Eric's hate-filled face haunted her. After a few minutes, she went inside.

The cool, semi-darkness of the big reception hall was a somber contrast to the warm sunshine outside. She remembered William Collins' suggestion that she study the portrait of the first Barnabas Collins and scanned the shadowed walls until she discovered the painting.

Moving closer, she was startled by the dark, handsome face that gazed down at her. It could have been the Barnabas she'd met the previous night, so identical was he in features to his long-dead ancestor.

The painting intrigued her and she remained there for some minutes. She was so absorbed by it that she was unaware she was no longer alone, until she turned to start up the broad stairway and found Eric standing there with his hand on the bannister. He was just a few steps from the bottom.

Now his hatred was replaced by derision. He said, "What a touching scene! You standing before the portrait of the first Barnabas with a rapt look of devotion!"

She blushed at his jeering remark. "I was only studying the portrait."

He came down another step towards her. "I think you're mooning over my cousin from England. Is it because he's English that you are drawn to him?"

"I'd rather not discuss that," she said, starting up the stairs and trying to avoid him.

Eric reached out and caught her by the wrist. A cynical smile showed on his face. "If you're tired of your sick husband don't waste time on Barnabas. I'm the most interesting man around here!"

"Please!" she cried angrily, wrenched her wrist free and hurried quickly up the stairs. His soft laughter followed her. At the door to her room, Ann paused to briefly collect herself. If things kept on like this, she would be forced to complain to her husband and find some other place to stay.

She opened the door and entered her room. Through the connecting door leading to John's room, she could see her gaunt husband nervously pacing up and down. The sight of him in such a mood alarmed her. Hesitantly, she went over to the doorway and stood watching him in silence.

A moment or so passed until he noticed her. Then he turned and halted, staring at her with his dark-circled eyes. "You're back," he said huskily.

"Yes. Are you all right?"

He stood in silence for a while, and then said, "I had a bad dream."

"Again?"

"Yes. It was so real I woke up and couldn't believe it had been a dream!" She could see he was trembling.

"Sit down and calm yourself," she said, as she led him to an easy chair by the window.

He sat in it heavily and then looked up at her in despair. "It's a dream I've had before. It comes to me over and over again."

Kneeling by him, Ann continued to hold one of his hands. The tremor racking his gaunt frame was alarmingly evident, yet it was nothing new to her. She had often paused in her duties in hospital wards to soothe the same kind of shell shock victim—but it was painfully different when the patient was your beloved husband.

"Erase the dream from your mind," she told him. "If it was unpleasant, try not to think of it."

He stared at her piteously. "I can't help thinking about it. It frightens me!"

She sighed. Trying another approach to help him, she suggested, "Then why not tell me about the dream so it won't seem so bad to you."

John's fine but ravaged face showed sudden fear. "I don't dare tell it to you!" he protested.

Ann was startled. "Why not?"

"You'd hate me," her husband said brokenly.

"Nothing would make me do that," she chided him. "And you shouldn't need me to remind you of it."

John turned to stare out the window at the chestnut trees in full foliage. A breeze whistled gently through them and their rustling became a kind of sigh. His shoulders had the limp slump of hopelessness that she always feared in patients.

He said, "The dream terrifies me. I'm afraid one day it will come true."

"Go on," she said.

John turned back to her. "It begins with us having a quarrel. I accuse you of paying too much attention to some other man. You say some terrible things to me... and then I come after you."

"Well?" she said, careful to keep her tone casual, though what he had said frightened her.

He licked his dry lips nervously. "After that I chase you for what seems a long time. In some dark place. And then I catch you and I find your throat and I choke you. You scream while you can, but after a while you're silent— silent because you're dead. But I keep on choking you. I can't stop! Then I wake up!" His voice had risen as he seemed to experience the horror of it all over again.

"You've had this dream several times before?" she asked in a dry voice.

"Yes. I can't stand it!" The trembling ran through him again.

"John, it's only a dream," she said softly. "Nothing that should alarm you or make you feel like this. It's something that never happened and never will happen!"

His sunken eyes held terror as they met hers. "That's it! That's what you don't understand!"

She thought she did, but it was necessary to pretend differently. "What don't I understand?"

"That it could happen!" he burst out. "That some time I could become so confused that I'd act out my dream and really strangle you!"

Ann tried not to think about the times when he'd attempted to kill her in his delirium. With a deep sigh, she said, "Now you're being needlessly concerned."

"No!" he protested. "You know how I am when I have my blackouts!"

"But you're not having them nearly so often," she said. "You're getting a lot better."

John bowed his head in despair. "Not when I have such dreams!"

"I say you are improving," she said quietly. "You must believe it."

"I'm frightened… frightened of what I may do to you!"

"I can take care of myself."

"It's all mixed up in my mind," he went on in deep anguish. "Perhaps I should be put away somewhere, like so many of the others."

Visions of mental wards with trembling, empty-eyed wrecks shuffling through them passed in her mind. Not for her husband! Never! She kissed him gently on the cheek and tasted the salt of the tears there. "You're going to be all right," she said. "Here in this quiet place you'll find your health. Now you must forget about this nonsense and get dressed for dinner."

After a few minutes, she convinced him to shave and change into a suit. She went to her room and began her own preparations for going down to join the others. As she sat before the mirror she thought of John's account of his dream. She'd been terrified by what he'd told her but hadn't dared let him know how she felt. It could be a sign that his mental state was getting worse.

She wouldn't believe that. She had to help him fight off the phantoms of his mind. One thing was clear: she couldn't confide her uneasiness about the old mansion to him. It would also be completely unwise for her to reveal Eric's overtures. A thing like that might really edge him on to madness. She would have to pretend that all was well and somehow suffer through the days and nights until their new home was ready.

Ann hoped that Barnabas might be a help to her in this crisis. Despite what the stern William Collins had said about the charming Englishman, she had felt an instant warmth for him. If she were lucky, he'd turn up after dinner.

John handled himself well during the evening meal. She was impressed by his control and his polite conversation. It was true John said nothing unless he was spoken to, but the mere fact he could offer credible replies indicated he was trying hard to fight his screaming nerves. Ann thought she was actually more tense then her husband.

They all gathered in the big living room after dinner. As darkness approached, a male servant came in and touched a flame to the lamp wicks of the overhead crystal chandeliers. The light that resulted from the rare cut glass chandeliers was soft and flattering.

William Collins addressed himself to Ann. "Tomorrow, the ladies of the village are having their annual garden party at the church grounds. I'd like you and John to attend as my guests."

"It sounds pleasant," she said. "We'd be happy to attend, as long as John is well enough."

"We'll trust that he will be," William said.

Eric gave John a meaningful glance. "I don't think you should miss it," he said mockingly. "I hear that Simeon Hale is providing a violin solo for the occasion. You remember Simeon, don't you?"

John paled. "Yes," he said in a low voice.

Eric smiled wisely. "Or perhaps it was Susan you knew the best?"

Ann sensed there was some double meaning to this question and quickly noted that John looked stricken. Anxious to protect him, she told Eric, "Is it necessary to bring up personalities in this fashion? Because of John's illness, it's not good for him to try and remember people."

Eric kept smiling. "I'm sure he remembers Susan without difficulty, don't you, John?"

"I'd rather not discuss that," John said stiffly. He turned to Ann and asked, "Wouldn't you like a stroll outside?"

"I'm sure it would be good for both of us." She smiled politely at the two Collins men. "If you'll kindly excuse us."

"Of course," William said. Eric merely showed silent amusement.

Ann quickly went out into the pleasant night air with her husband. There were a myriad of stars in the sky above, the fragrance of June filled the night. They walked across the lawn.

"Eric can be unpleasant when he likes," she ventured.

"Yes," John said distantly.

"But you mustn't allow him to bother you."

"He does that deliberately," John said with bitterness.

"Who is that Simeon Hale he mentioned?"

"The church organist and town music teacher," John said quietly.

"Why did he bring his name up? And that of his sister?" Ann asked.

John didn't answer, but stared directly ahead, far out across the bay and murmured, "I may have made a bad mistake in coming back here and building a house."

"Why do you say that?" she asked, studying his tense profile.

"Hayward brides are safer away from Collinsport."

"That's not your real reason," she protested. "You've already told me you don't believe in that legend."

"I could change my mind."

"But you haven't," she said. "Something else made you say that, and it has to be connected with what Eric said a few minutes ago." She hesitated. "Were you ever in love with the Susan Hale he mentioned?"

He gave her a startled look. "Why do you ask that?"

"It would be the most obvious thing for Eric to hint," she said with some bitterness. "He has a nasty, small, mind!"

"I'm going inside," John said, looking uneasy.

"I'll go with you," she said.

"No!" he almost shouted. "I'd rather go alone. I want to go up to my room and rest some more."

Ann studied him anxiously in the near-darkness. "I don't think you should be alone."

"I want to be alone," John insisted. "If I feel better I'll come back and join you here shortly."

She had no opportunity to argue with him further. He had already turned and was firmly striding towards the house. She worried about what kind of row he might get into in there, then decided there wouldn't be any real battle, since John wasn't well enough to carry on a quarrel. He would undoubtedly go straight up to his room.

Standing there with a feeling of uncertainty, she came to the reluctant conclusion she'd better give him his way and allow him to be alone for a little. Her anger at Eric and his taunting continued to grow. She felt he hated both her and John, and was trying to destroy them.

With a tiny shudder she glanced along the cliffs and saw a blurred figure coming slowly towards her. At first she was frightened, but then, as the person came closer, she saw that it was Barnabas. In his caped-coat he made an imposing appearance.

He stood before her in the blue shadows of the summer night. A faint smile played across his handsome face. "We meet again."

"Yes. I've wanted to talk with you."

"Good."

"I tried to reach you this afternoon."

"That would be doomed to failure," he said gently.

"I got nowhere," she admitted. "I didn't understand your need for privacy during the day."

"It happens to be one of my burdens," Barnabas said. "But I'm here now and at your service. How are you making out here?"

Ann glanced worriedly at the lights of the great mansion a distance behind them. "Collinwood is not a happy place for us."

"Indeed? Why not?"

Her eyes met his. "I'd think you could guess," she said. "It's Eric."

"I'm not surprised," Barnabas said.

"He's tried to impose himself on me and he delights in taunting both myself and John. I wouldn't mind for myself, but John is still very sick and his nerves can't stand the torment."

"Have you told Eric that?"

"Yes," she said bitterly, "but he pays no attention to it. His father has ruined him! He's the most selfish, most spoiled person I've ever met."

"William never recovered from the death of Eric's brother, Tom. And since then he's been much too indulgent with his remaining son."

"There's no question about that," she said angrily. "I don't know what I'll do but I doubt we can remain here, unless he stops his hatefulness."

Barnabas sighed. "Perhaps if I spoke to him…"

"I doubt if it would help," she worried. "He's already made it clear he thinks I favor you, and has shown jealousy over it."

"Interesting," Barnabas said.

She gazed up at the man in the caped coat. "Eric doesn't seem to believe it possible I love my husband because he happens to be ill. His illness is one of my reasons for caring for him. I saw so many boys like him."

"I think I understand," Barnabas said gently.

"If you visited any of those service hospitals in England you must know," she said brokenly. "I had to save John."

"It seems you've done very well."

She shook her head. "He's not safe yet, and he'll have a relapse unless he's removed from any tensions."

"Collinwood is a house of tension."

"I'm discovering that too late," she admitted. "I can see that he's reverting to his old state and we've only been here a short time. Just a little while ago Eric upset him by mentioning a Simeon Hale."

Barnabas frowned. "What did he say about Hale?"

"He's playing a violin solo for some garden party tomorrow that we're supposed to attend. Eric suggested that John would be pleased to meet Simeon Hale again."

Barnabas sighed. "I doubt that."

"And he also spoke of Hale's sister, a girl named Susan."

"How did John react to that?"

"Badly," she said. "Was there a love affair between John and that girl? Will she be at the garden party tomorrow?"

"No," Barnabas said quietly, "she won't be there."

"I wish she would come. I'd like to talk to her," Ann said.

"That might be difficult," Barnabas said with a cryptic smile. "Susan Hale is dead."

CHAPTER 5

"Dead!" Ann gasped.

"Yes," Barnabas nodded solemnly. "Eric knows all about that. Without a question, it is why he mentioned the name of her and her brother."

"To hurt my husband?"

"Presumably," he answered.

"What is the full story?"

Barnabas hesitated. "Perhaps it would be better if you closed your mind to the subject. Just forgot you ever heard the name Hale."

She gave him a bitter look. "I'm afraid Eric has ruined any likelihood of that. I wish you'd tell me the truth."

"Very well," Barnabas agreed. "Several years ago, John and Susan Hale were engaged. Then the engagement was suddenly broken. A little later Susan Hale was swimming near her home and drowned. She was a good swimmer and it was a calm, clear day. No one could understand it. And so the rumor began that she had deliberately allowed herself to drown because she was heartbroken over her quarrel with John."

Ann was badly upset by the story and gave Barnabas a searching look. "Do you think there is any basis for the rumor?"

"No," he said. "It's my guess the girl suffered some kind of attack and would have drowned in any case."

"Does John believe that?"

"I think so," Barnabas said. "He was saddened by the girl's death but very sensible about it. It was Simeon Hale, her brother, who took it very badly. He's a sensitive young man and his entire life seems to have been built around his sister. He keeps to himself a good deal and aside from playing the organ at the church, the villagers see little of him. He took the stand John was directly responsible for his sister's death, and made several threats against him."

"This must have made it very difficult for my husband," Ann worried.

"It did," Barnabas agreed. "I think it was the deciding factor in his leaving here. Then the war came along, and you know the rest."

"If John goes to that garden party tomorrow he'll be exposed to Simeon Hale again," she said.

"I don't think there will be any trouble." Barnabas told her. "Enough time has passed. I think the sting of Susan's death no longer torments Simeon. Of course, with a type like that, you can never be positive."

"Eric would encourage him to make a scene, if he could," she said with bitterness.

"I wouldn't worry about it," Barnabas advised. "I'm sure John can handle Simeon."

"John isn't as well as he was when he left here," she reminded him.

"Everything has changed and time has passed," he said. "I'd count on Simeon no longer being in a vengeful mood."

"I hope that's the way it turns out, if we should go. I'll try to avoid it, but William Collins can be very insistent."

Barnabas gave her one of his melancholy smiles. "I know that."

"He also gave me a lecture about you," she said.

"That doesn't surprise me."

She frowned. "Why doesn't he approve of you? He can't really believe those fantastic stories linking you with an ancestor who was a vampire."

"William has a touchy disposition and a great sense of responsibility towards the people of the village. Sometimes he becomes overly concerned," Barnabas answered.

"I think you are being very fair, perhaps too fair," she said.

"William doesn't understand me," Barnabas said. "And whatever he doesn't understand, makes him suspicious. It's as simple as that."

"I have felt from the first I could count on you," Ann said.

"And you can," he promised.

"I met that man with the black bandage down one side of his face," Ann told him. "His name is Warren Miller. He used to be an actor."

Barnabas eyed her with interest. "Is that what he told you?"

"Yes," she said. "Isn't it the truth?"

"Not completely," he said.

"He seemed a very pleasant man, a little reserved because he's aware of his appearance."

"I have learned some things about this Miller," Barnabas said quietly. "I'm not at liberty to reveal them yet. When I do, they may surprise you."

"Collinwood has been a place of surprises," she said ruefully, "and not all of them pleasant."

"I can understand that."

"It seems I may be foolish in staying on here," she worried.

Barnabas told her, "I'd like you to stay. Your problems may well be solved by meeting them head-on. And you can do that best at Collinwood."

"Eric makes it much more difficult than it otherwise would be," she pointed out.

"He'll bear watching," Barnabas agreed. "But I'm sure you can count on the fairness and honesty of his father."

Ann sighed deeply and turned to stare across at the big house which stood against the star-filled sky, its great, dark bulk somewhat menacing. "I think we made a mistake coming here. I had no idea John was so ill." Briefly, without too much detail, she let Barnabas know how she'd been attacked in the night, and how she suspected John had been responsible. With a wry smile, she finished, "It was either him or one of Collinwood's famed ghosts."

"I wouldn't rule out the second possibility," Barnabas advised.

"It would almost please me to think it was a ghost," she said. "But the evidence against John is strong. The recurrent nightmare he has of strangling me terrifies both of us."

Barnabas frowned. "You think the nightmare could well be a prelude to reality?"

"Yes."

"You should have John see the doctor in town," he suggested. "He might be able to give him something to make him sleep."

"I intend to do that," Ann said. "But so much has happened since we arrived."

"Don't be afraid to attend the garden party tomorrow," Barnabas told her. "In fact, Dr. Stair may be there. He's a pleasant old man and he often attends such functions."

"Is he a good doctor?"

"Good enough. He has had plenty of local experience. He

probably has been John's doctor since he was a child, so he should know him well enough, even if he isn't familiar with the shell shock condition."

"That's true," she agreed, feeling better.

"I'll walk you to the house," Barnabas said. "It's not wise for you to venture out after dark on your own. Strange things are taking place in this area."

She gave him a wistful smile. "So William Collins suggested when he warned me about you."

Barnabas laughed softly. "Perhaps you should keep his warning in mind. I may not be as trustworthy as you suppose."

"I'll still defend you against the charge of being a vampire," she said.

Barnabas took her by the arm as he escorted her across the broad lawn to Collinwood. "Your confidence is warming," he said. "I'll try to justify it, and I'll give you some sound advice. If you meet Warren Miller again, don't allow yourself to become too friendly with him."

"You make it sound as if he were dangerous. He seemed so mild-mannered and pleasant."

"I have my reasons for saying what I have," Barnabas assured her

"Very well," she said. "I'll be careful."

"Don't make it appear you are afraid of him," the man at her side warned further. "I don't want him to know he's being watched."

"Is he?"

"Yes," Barnabas said emphatically. "I'm making it a personal project to find out more about this wounded war veteran."

They had reached the front entrance of Collinwood but Ann was unwilling to say goodnight to Barnabas. She had no idea what kind of mood John would be in.

Glancing towards the house, she said, "I'm reluctant to go in there."

"That's too bad," he sympathized.

"I'm afraid of Collinwood and what it may do to us," she said with a small shiver.

"Fight the evil," he advised.

"It may not be easy," she said.

"It rarely is," he agreed. "But I have an idea you can master it. Besides, your own place will soon be finished."

"I'm counting on that," Ann sighed.

"The days will go quickly," Barnabas said. "Until I see you again, good luck!"

"Will you be around tomorrow night?" she asked, anxiously.

"If I can," he said, his handsome face shadowing. "It's not

always easy for me to make plans."

"It means a lot to me to be able to see you regularly, and to talk to you," she confided.

Barnabas pressed her arm gently. "I'll not forget about you. I promise you that."

She left him standing there, and she went on into the house. As soon as she stepped inside, the eerie silence made her uneasy. All the lights were out downstairs, except for a night lamp in an alcove over the stairway. Its murky light barely illuminated the stairs, and by the time she reached the landing at the second floor, everything was all shadow and darkness.

Her hand still on the railing, Ann hesitated for a moment before making her way along the corridor to her rooms. Where could all the others have gone? she wondered. Was it usual for this strange household to retire at such an early hour?

Suddenly, she heard something that sent a sickening chill through her. From the dark shadows on the landing to her left came the sound of heavy breathing. A tortured sound! She stared in the direction from which it came, but she saw nothing but the menacing darkness! Then the breathing seemed to stop.

A door slammed far down the other corridor, followed by a frightening silence. She stood there, waiting and listening, hardly daring to venture the short distance to her door. But she knew that the black hallway had to be braved, and she might as well make a start. Drawing on all her courage, Ann let go of the railing and slowly walked into the shadows.

When she was partway down the hall, she was certain she heard a footstep a short distance behind her. Or was it the creaking of a board, caused by her own progress along the dark corridor? She couldn't really be sure, but she hastened her pace until she came to her own door. With a deep feeling of relief, she opened it and went inside.

But now she was faced with a new ordeal. Standing in the glow of soft lamplight was a hollow-eyed John. He'd changed into pajamas and dressing gown, and was now facing her with an accusing look on his thin face.

"I didn't know you'd still be up."

His eyes narrowed. "Didn't you want to see me?"

"Of course," she said quickly. "But you complained of being ill when you left me out on the lawn. I thought you'd go straight to bed."

"I didn't," he said.

"I can see that," she answered quietly, trying to judge his mood, uneasy lest he be slipping into one of his demented spells.

His burning eyes fixed on her. "Who were you with just now?"

"Outside?"

"Yes. I saw you from the window. Someone walked across the lawn with you."

"That was Barnabas," she said. "He came to me on the cliff after you left. He didn't want me to walk back by myself."

"Very thoughtful of him," her husband said with sarcasm.

She frowned. "Surely you can't resent his trying to take care of me."

"I don't imagine he had to be coaxed," John said, his tone harsh. Ann saw that he was trembling slightly. "Or maybe you did coax him?"

She felt her cheeks burn. "If you weren't ill I'd not forgive you for saying a thing like that," she told him. "But I know it's your illness and not you talking."

"Don't be too certain!" he snapped.

"Go to bed!" she pleaded. "In the morning you'll feel better."

"Now you're treating me like a crazy man," John said, his hands clenching and unclenching nervously.

Ann kept a brave front, but she was thinking of the dream he had had, in which they quarreled and he ended by strangling her. She was beginning to fear this might be the start of such an angry scene.

"You're being unreasonably touchy and stupidly jealous," she remarked calmly. "I'm the last person to ever describe you as crazy. And Barnabas is our friend."

"Barnabas was ordered away from Collinsport by his own family more than once," John said. "Ask him about the village girls!"

"I don't need to do that," she declared. "I've heard the rumors and I don't believe them."

"Because he's talked you into being on his side," her husband said. "He's got a sly tongue."

"That's not so," she said. "I think the things they say against him are ridiculous exaggerations. And if you'll be fair, you'll agree."

"It was common talk," John declared. "Long before I left here."

Ann felt she must use some shock method to try and get him off this, so with quiet defiance she told him, "I suppose the rumors were as fair as the ones they spread about you and Susan Hale, when they claimed your quarrel with her was responsible for her suicide. That her drowning wasn't an accident!"

It shocked him out of his angry, accusing mood. Now he looked at her in a dazed fashion. "Where did you hear that story?"

"It also has gone the rounds of the village," she said.

The hollow-eyes of her husband showed fear. "It's a pack of lies. I don't know what happened to Susan but I'm sure it wasn't the fault of any quarrel we had. We broke up by mutual agreement."

"I believe you," she said. "Just as I feel you should be willing to believe that Barnabas isn't guilty of having the vampire taint. If the rumors about you are groundless, why shouldn't they also be unfounded in his case?"

A contrite look crossed her husband's face. "I'm sorry," he said.

"You should be."

John came close to her, a study in anguish. "I know I wasn't being fair. But my head aches and I get mixed up. You mean everything to me and seeing him with you made me jealous."

"You never need be jealous," she told him.

"I try to remember that," he said unhappily. "But I'm too confused."

She touched a hand to his arm. "It's all right. Now you really should get some rest."

"I will," he promised. And with a look of infinite sadness on his thin face, he took her in his arms for a goodnight kiss. The moment of tenderness between them eased some of her fear. When he let her go, he said. "You made a mistake in marrying me. You must realize that."

"Why?"

"Whether either of us want to admit it or not, I'm far from normal," he confessed brokenly. "My nerves are shattered."

"You're getting better. Your nerves are healing."

"Not enough," he said. "I'm far from well. And I'm frightened. This village and this house frighten me. The idea of a meeting tomorrow with Simeon Hale frightens me. He's a neurotic and he blames me for what happened to his sister."

"It's one of the things you must face, for your own sake," she told him. "Your ability to meet such a situation could be a milestone of your recovery."

John sighed. "Perhaps it will rain. The garden party may be cancelled and then we needn't worry about attending."

"Perhaps," she said. "I don't think it is all that important."

After John had returned to his room, Ann slowly began to prepare for bed. The situation between them was becoming increasingly difficult, and she could see that he needed medical care—as soon as possible. The obsession that she was betraying him with some other man had taken a firm grip on his sick mind, and went deeper than he realized. Not much was required for the obsession to change to outright madness.

Her own nervous state was deteriorating, which could have unfortunate results for both of them because she had to take on so many of his problems. The antagonism John felt for Barnabas was especially unfortunate, since the charming Britisher could be their best bastion against the dangers that beset them. She had to try and make her husband see things more rationally, and she had to keep the trouble-making Eric from agitating him needlessly.

With this decided, she closed her eyes and soon dropped off to sleep. It was a deep, dreamless slumber, but before long, a weird kind of howling penetrated her sleeping state and woke her with a start. The eerie howls had not been imaginary. She was wide awake now and could still hear them. She got out of bed and hastily put on her slippers and went to the window to try and see if the cries were from one of the dogs she'd encountered on the big estate.

Ann peered down into the garden, but she was unable to see anything. The howling stopped for a moment, then began again. Now Ann was thoroughly alarmed. Glancing into her husband's room, she saw that he was still asleep. Luckily the wolf cries, for that is what they seemed to be, had not made him wake up.

Now she heard a new burst of eerie howling. This time she was actually able to see the creature. It was large and a yellowish-gray. As she watched, it quickly ran off and vanished behind some hedges. The idea of a wolf on the grounds of Collinwood shocked her. There had to be some strange explanation for its presence in the garden. Her own theory was almost as outrageous as some of the things she'd heard about Barnabas.

Someone had mentioned that Collinwood had been haunted by a werewolf. Why shouldn't this explain what she'd just seen? This was no ordinary animal, and Ann was convinced it must be linked with the supernatural. When she saw Barnabas again, she would question him about this. She remained at the window for minutes longer, but there were no further cries nor any sign of the giant wolf-like creature.

Nothing else interrupted her sleep. The balance of the night passed peacefully. She had hoped the day would be wet or at least dark and threatening, but it wasn't. The sun was shining brightly. When John joined her, already dressed for the day, she gave him a wry smile. "It seems your prayers for rain weren't answered."

He scowled out the window at the sunshine. "It had to be a perfect day."

"So we will be attending the garden party."

"I haven't said I'd go," he hedged. "We'll see what it's like later."

"You know that William Collins expects us to attend," she said. "And we owe him some consideration as his guests. I don't think you should allow that dead girl's brother to scare you away."

"That's not it!" John protested, but he didn't sound convincing.

After breakfast, Ann went for a walk along the cliffs, to the area known as Widows' Hill. It was the high point of the cliffs and from this vantage spot, you had the best view of the surrounding countryside. There was a bench there, and when she reached it she was mildly surprised to discover Warren Miller seated there.

He rose to greet her. "Good morning," he said.

"Good morning," she replied, noting the almost handsome face marred by the black silk bandage and dark glasses. "I didn't notice you were here until I came close."

He smiled faintly. "I admit to being a trespasser."

"I'm sure William Collins wouldn't consider you that."

"Don't take it for granted," he said. "Actually, that is what I am, but I couldn't resist discovering what the view was like from up here."

"Isn't it lovely," she said, studying the bay and the points of land at each end of it.

"A delightful place," the former actor said. "For a little while, I forgot about my own woes."

"It is a calm, perfect day."

Warren Miller was watching her closely. "Have you had any other strange accidents since your nasty one of the other day?"

She shook her head. "No."

"Fortunate for you," he said suavely. "I always feel such accidents don't happen singly. They usually come in a series of two or three."

"I hope not," she said.

"So do I," the tall, sedate man said.

Ann couldn't help wondering what it was Barnabas suspected about him, what his secret might be. For her own part, she thought he was a harmless figure, but she would heed the warning of the Britisher.

She said, "Why don't you stroll back to Collinwood with me and meet some of the others? My husband would be glad to know you. He's a war veteran too. And like you, he still isn't himself."

"I hope it isn't as obvious as it is in my case," Warren said, indicating the black silk bandage.

"He has no outward scars," she said. "But the scars on his brain are equally tragic. He was shell-shocked."

"That is a nasty business."

She sighed. "So you see you are not alone in having a burden to bear."

"I understand that," he said. "I still would prefer to remain apart from Collinwood for the time being. But I trust your husband and I may meet out here, or perhaps along the beach, one day."

"I'll mention that to him," she promised.

"Watch yourself in that old mansion," he added. "I have always suspected that it harbors evil spirits."

"Then you do know it?"

He nodded. "Very well."

"You visited it before the war when you came here?"

"Yes."

"This is my first time here. It's quite an experience," she said. "I'm sorry now we didn't make arrangements to stay at the hotel, but it would be awkward for us to leave so soon after arriving. I hope we may manage it later, on the grounds the place isn't good for my husband's nerves."

"I'm sure it isn't," Warren agreed.

She sighed. "Something strange has happened since I saw you. Last night I was wakened by an eerie howling. When I went to the window, I saw a huge wolf-like animal on the lawn."

"There are no wolves in this part of Maine," he said.

"That's why I'm so puzzled," she agreed. "There has to be an explanation."

"You were probably not fully awake, and in the near darkness, you mistakenly decided the animal was larger than it really was."

"It could have happened that way," she admitted. "But it didn't."

"Sure?"

"Yes. I think what I saw one of the Collinwood ghosts you're always hinting about."

"I don't recall mentioning that kind of phantom."

Ann said, "I'm sure you did. It's the werewolf the villagers claim roamed the estate."

The actor arched his eyebrow. "Do you accept there are such things as werewolves?"

"After last night, I'm beginning to believe in them. Probably what I saw was the ghost of one. I'm sure it was a supernatural creature."

"I can see that you are falling victim to the phantoms of that old mansion," he chided. "The spell of the place is working on you."

She stared at him with some dismay. "You don't think the atmosphere of Collinwood is actually making me imagine such things?"

"Yes. And I warn you this could only be a beginning," Warren said with some earnestness. "All the tragedy that has taken place within those walls will gradually make itself felt by you. You will be caught up in it like the helpless insect that falls victim to a spider's web!"

She listened in frightened fascination. "You make it seem so convincing."

"What I'm saying is the truth," he told her solemnly. "If you ask Barnabas Collins, he'll tell you the same thing."

"Do you know Barnabas well?"

"Only by sight," he said vaguely.

"He has spoken to me of you."

"He can't have more than mentioned me," Warren said. "We've not had any conversations."

"You should talk with him. He's very nice."

The half-face showed a twisted smile. "You're an extremely naive young woman, I fear. You're too ready to accept anyone as a pleasant individual. That could lead you into serious trouble."

She gave him a skeptical look. "Barnabas told me almost that same thing."

"So you have two mentors," Warren Miller said. "It would be wise to listen to one of us."

"I'll consider it," she promised as she saw a change of expression on his part. "What's wrong?" she asked.

"I've stayed too long, talking to you," Warren said. "We are about to be joined by a third party I'd rather not meet!"

CHAPTER 6

Ann turned to see who this third party might be and at once recognized the erect figure of William Collins coming towards them from the direction of the big mansion. He was striding along briskly, his cane flicking in the air at set intervals. The grim expression on his angular face showed that he was determined to reach them before Warren Miller had a chance to retreat.

Ann looked at the war veteran again. "You needn't worry about him. He's really a nice old man."

"Perhaps," Warren said in a tense voice. "But I still would have preferred to avoid him."

"It's probably a good thing for you two to meet," she said. "It will make it easier for you to visit Collinwood."

William Collins approached them, slightly out of breath, and addressed himself to Ann first. "I saw you here, talking with someone. I decided to find out who our visitor was." He glanced at the former actor questioningly.

Ann spoke up for Warren Miller. "This is the young man who has rented the beach cottage," she said, and made the proper introductions.

William Collins offered his hand to the younger man. "I've heard several people mention you," he said. "I wondered how long it would be before we'd meet."

Warren looked unhappy as he shook hands with the squire

of Collinwood. "I hadn't intended to be an interloper," he said. "I was beguiled up here by a desire to sample the view."

"You are welcome to visit the estate whenever you like," William Collins said. "We are always anxious to be on good terms with our neighbors. Have you met my son, Eric?"

"No," Warren answered.

"He's about your age," William Collins said. "Interested in horses and racing. If you enjoy riding, he'd be glad to supply you with a mount any time. He is anxious to have them exercised."

"I'll remember that," Warren said rather nervously. "Thank you. And now if you'll both excuse me, I must be on my way."

He nodded to Ann and at once left them and hurried along the cliff path to a place where he could take another path down to the beach. She saw that William Collins was watching the vanishing figure with a slight frown on his lined face.

"Strange thing," he observed.

"What?"

"That fellow. I have the impression that I should know him."

She said, "Perhaps you did meet before. He claims he came here as a summer visitor several years ago."

"I must have seen him then," the old man mused. "His voice had a familiar ring to it, as well."

"He's very shy because of his terrible disfigurement."

"Unfortunate," the old man agreed with a sigh.

"I hope that he will not keep so to himself now."

"No reason why he should. Everyone understands and sympathizes in a case of that kind," William Collins said.

"Perhaps that's his reason for desiring to keep to himself," she suggested. "He may wish to avoid sympathy."

"True. You make a good point."

As they began to walk back towards Collinwood, Ann took the opportunity of saying, "I'm not sure John should attend the garden party today."

Collins glanced at her with some surprise. "Why not?"

"It may be too much of a strain for him," she said.

He continued to seem puzzled. "Pleasant company, light food and drink in the outdoors, chance to meet old friends, should make it an ideal occasion."

"If John were well I'd be the first to agree," she said. "But he is still convalescing from his war injuries."

William Collins showed concern. "I keep forgetting that, of course," he apologized. "I leave it entirely with you, my dear, but I trust that you will attend. It would help make the party a success."

She smiled. "I doubt if that is true. But I will be there. I'd like to meet some of the village people—especially Dr. Stair."

"He should be there for a short time at least," Mr. Collins promised. "Of course he's busy since he's the only doctor we have here."

"So I understand," she said. "He must know John."

The old man chuckled. "Like as not he brought him into the world. You can ask him."

When they reached the house, she went upstairs at once. She found John slumped in an easy chair in his room. He wasn't reading, nor even looking out the window, but just sitting there staring blankly in front of him. His dismal state troubled her. She went over and stood by him. Her appearance roused him out of his abject mood.

Glancing up at her, he asked, "Where were you?"

"I walked as far as Widows' Hill. Then I came back with William Collins."

His eyes searched her face. "Where was Barnabas?"

"Not around. He works in the days." She didn't like this reference to Barnabas without any reason. It showed her husband's thinking was disjointed and confused.

He said, "I missed you."

"I thought you might come and join me," she said, "and then I decided you were resting for the party this afternoon."

"I'm not going to it," John said quickly, as if in fear she might try to make him.

Ann gave him a reassuring smile. "You needn't worry about it."

"No?" His tone was suspicious.

"No," she said. "I've talked to Mr. Collins and made him understand it would be too strenuous for you, so you don't have to go. I'll make an appearance and that will do."

"You're going?"

"Yes." She stared at him. "You don't object to that, do you?"

His hollow-eyes had a too-bright look. "It might be better if you didn't."

Ann knelt by his chair and looked into his face earnestly. "If I don't go either, Mr. Collins will really feel hurt. You must see that. I don't mind going and I think I should."

"I see." John gripped the arms of the chair tensely with his thin hands.

"Are you sure you understand?"

He was staring straight ahead again. "Yes."

"You don't mind?"

"No." He was hardly listening to her, lost in his own thoughts.

Ann sighed in relief. "Good. Then you mustn't worry about it. And you should take a long stroll outdoors when we're in the village. You need the fresh air and sunshine."

John didn't answer her, but she felt she shouldn't press him for a reply. There were times like this when she had to let him emerge slowly from his dark mood. He needed to be given complete freedom. To push him in any direction at such moments could be a serious mistake, so she left him sitting silently in the chair while she returned to her own room to dress for the afternoon.

She selected a white linen dress with a blue collar and a wide-brimmed straw hat with a blue band to protect her from the sun. When she went downstairs, she found Eric waiting for her.

"You look great," he said with a knowing smile. "Did you wear that outfit for me?"

"Not any more than you put on that tan suit and boater straw hat for me," she said derisively.

"But I am wearing them for you," he protested with a mocking smile, and he held up the flat-topped straw hat.

"Where's your father?" she asked.

"Outside, seeing about the car," Eric said. "He insisted on using it today. I'd much rather have taken the horses and carriage. But he's so proud of his new automobile he wouldn't think of going to the party in anything else."

"Are we to meet him outside?"

"He'll have Dawson bring it around," Eric told her. With another of his mocking looks, he said, "So I'm to have you all to myself today."

"I wouldn't count on that," she warned him. She was building a healthy dislike for the brash young man.

"Come now," he said. "Don't tell me you never look at anyone but that dour, sick husband of yours. You need a pleasant change once in a while."

"I'll decide when I do."

He stared at her. "What have you got against me?"

"You should know," she told him. "You've done everything you could to make me dislike you from the first moment we met."

Eric shook his head. "That's not true."

"And the other afternoon, when I was sitting in the garden, I happened to glance at the upstairs window and saw you there—with an expression of hatred on your face that actually scared me. Why do you dislike me so? And don't try to argue that you don't. I caught you off guard, and I know what was written on your face—sheer hatred!"

The young man listened to her outburst and then, his face crimson, said, "I don't remember it at all."

"You didn't know I'd seen you."

"I doubt that you did. You probably imagined it."

"Don't try to blame it on Collinwood's ghosts," she protested. "The pale, vicious face I saw appeared at a window in midafternoon. And it was you."

Eric looked uncomfortable. "If you're so positive there's no use my denying it."

"None at all!"

They might have gone on with this discussion had not the blaring horn of William Collins' auto attracted their attention to the front door. They went outside and joined him in the rear seat of the open touring car. He was wearing a dustcoat, cap and heavy-rimmed goggles. In the front seat, at the wheel, sat the stately Dawson. When Eric and Ann were safely seated beside him, Mr. Collins waved the chauffeur on.

The automobile sputtered and went forward at a slow, uneven, speed. Eric observed the performance of the vehicle glumly and said, "I'd have preferred the carriage."

His father glared at him. "You're only interested in showing off your horses."

"And you in showing off your car!" Eric shot back.

Ann sat between them and politely tried to ignore their arguments. She missed a good deal of what was said because of the noise of the engine and the wind that swept their voices away. She congratulated herself on having brought along a scarf, which she'd used to tie around her straw hat and keep it on her head.

After what seemed an age, they arrived at the church picnic grounds. A large crowd was already there. Within a few minutes Ann was introduced to at least a dozen people whose names she was unable to remember.

She was soon captured by a huge, imposing old woman who was a summer visitor. The big woman beamed at her over her tea cup, "And they tell me you were a nurse in the war?"

"Yes," Ann said, anxious to escape but not knowing how.

"What a lot of terrible things you must have seen!"

"Yes," she agreed weakly. She was looking for William Collins to rescue her, or at this point, even Eric!

"Dreadful injuries," the woman went on. "No one will ever know, I guess."

"True," Ann replied absently.

"I hear there's one poor chap staying at a cottage near the beach," the old woman confided. "They tell me that his face was shot away and he's really a horror to look at!"

Ann was disgusted. She gave her captor an angry glance.

"I've met the young man you're talking about," she said. "He's very nice, and aside from concealing his most serious injuries with a black bandage, he has a pleasant face."

"Oh?" She looked and sounded disappointed.

Ann couldn't resist continuing. "My own husband also happens to be a war casualty, so you will understand I'm very familiar with such things."

"Dear me!" The big woman looked aghast. "I'm sorry!" And she turned and hurried off.

"What did you say to Mrs. Devlin to send her off so quickly, I'd like to find out for my own information?" a cheery, elderly male voice put the question to her.

She turned to see a short man with white whiskers and twinkling blue eyes. "I'm afraid I had to be blunt with her."

"The best treatment, I promise you," he chuckled. "She is not one of my favorite summer ladies."

Ann smiled at him. "You sound suspiciously like a native."

"I am," he said. "You're English and married to John Hayward, and you're staying at Collinwood while your new house is being built."

"You know everything?" she marveled.

"I have a fair supply of knowledge," he said modestly. "I'm Dr. Stair and I'm glad to meet you."

Ann brightened. "I'm delighted to meet you, Doctor," she said. "I've been wanting to talk to you about John. I assume he was once a patient of yours."

"From the day of his birth," the doctor said proudly. "Is he somewhere around?"

"No," she sighed. "I decided he shouldn't come."

"Oh?"

"You may have heard he was badly shell-shocked."

He raised his white eyebrows. "Is that what it was? I knew he'd been injured, but didn't hear the details. Well, that's serious enough."

Ann was showing her worry now. "His is a bad case, and since we've gotten here, I'm afraid he's become worse."

"You should be familiar with the symptoms. You were a nurse in the field."

"Yes," she agreed. "He's having blackout spells and occasional fits of delirium."

"Sounds bad."

"It's not that bad," she defended John, but knowing she was probably wrong in her optimism. "But he's been having one unpleasant dream, night after night. I think he needs a sedative to break the sequence of the dream. Then perhaps after a few good nights of sleep, he might not remember it."

The white-whiskered doctor nodded. "That is a possibility."

"Will you see him?"

"Yes," Dr. Stair readily agreed. "I'll be out that way tomorrow, likely in the early afternoon. I'll call by to see him if you like, though I'm no specialist in his trouble."

"Thank you," she said. "I'd really appreciate it."

As she spoke, a dried-up looking man with the face of a grim fanatic and the long, brown hair of a musician appeared with a violin. He stood bleakly, ignoring the gathering, as one of the committee ladies came forward and introduced him.

"Mr. Simeon Hale will now kindly play a violin solo for us," she gushed.

Dr. Stair nudged Ann. "Have you met him yet?"

"No."

The old man gave her an enquiring glance. "You know who he is?"

"Yes. John was once engaged to his sister."

Dr. Stair nodded. "I see you've heard the story. Bad news travels fast. Simeon Hale really gave your John a bad time after his sister was drowned. It was completely unfair of him."

"So I've heard," she said.

"But he happens to be a good musician," he admitted grudgingly.

As if to prove this point, Simeon Hale began to play. He did have an excellent, strong tone and a good technique. He held the attention of the crowd for a short, light classic. Then he played an equally short encore and with a bow, vanished from the central area where he'd been playing.

Dr. Stair gave Ann a knowing look. "Talent and madness sometimes go hand in hand, and there's an example."

"He played beautifully."

"Yes," the doctor admitted glumly. "I wish that is all there was to him. Just his music."

At that point Eric Collins came over to them and gave Ann a teasing look. "I just did you a favor. I pointed you out as John's wife to Simeon Hale."

Dr. Stair looked angry. "That was a silly thing to do."

Eric looked smug. "I like to keep things moving."

The doctor looked resigned. "I can't say I approve of your methods." Turning to Ann, he said, "I have to leave now, Mrs. Hayward, but I'll look in on your husband at Collinwood tomorrow afternoon."

"We'll be expecting you, Doctor," she said.

As soon as the white-whiskered little man left them, Eric told her airily, "He's pretty limited—just the local doctor. Whenever one of us is really ill, we send to Ellsworth or Bangor for the doctors there."

Ann said, "He strikes me as being intelligent."

"Just a country doctor," Eric insisted.

"I've known some of them to be near-geniuses," she said. "Did he look after your brother when he was so ill?"

Eric frowned. "No. Dad sent Tom to a hospital in Boston."

"Still, I understand he died, which proves that even Boston doctors and hospitals have their limitations."

"No one said they didn't," Eric replied. "It seems to me you like to start arguments about nothing."

"Sorry," she smiled bleakly. "We don't seem to get on too well."

"That isn't my fault," Eric said, and with a dark look her way, left.

Ann wasn't upset by his leaving. She found it difficult to talk with him, and it was hard to conceal her dislike for him. She was beginning to tire of the party and wished that William Collins would come and suggest they return home. She was also worried about John. She didn't like him being left alone too much.

All at once she was conscious of someone standing close to her. She turned and found herself face to face with Simeon Hale. He gave her a cold look and said, "I understand you are Mrs. John Hayward."

"Yes," she said quietly.

"How does it feel to be the wife of a murderer?"

Ann stared at him, her mouth gaping open. "I don't think I heard you right."

His steel gray eyes glittered like those of a snake. "I think you did," he said precisely. "Do you enjoy being married to a killer?"

"You must be insane!"

He smiled nastily. "That's no answer to my questions."

"They don't deserve an answer," she protested angrily.

"I felt I should meet you as soon as I knew who you were."

Ann felt faint. "Please leave me. If you don't, I'll call on someone for help."

"I wouldn't advise it," the wizened-faced musician said. "It would only cause the talk to start all over again. And while that couldn't hurt my poor sister now, it might be very unpleasant for you!"

"I know who you are and that you have mistaken ideas about my husband," she told him. "John did not cause your sister's death. He's much too kind to hurt anyone."

"You're wrong about that," the madman said softly. "He killed Susan, all right. And he'll pay."

"You're insane!"

"I could be. I have suffered enough through Susan's tragic death. But I'm going to feel better shortly. And can you guess why? Because I'm going to make your husband pay for what he did."

"John did nothing."

"We disagree on that point, Mrs. Hayward. But I'm sure we both do agree on one point: He loves you. And perhaps through you I can bring him the same hurt he brought me. Think about that, Mrs. Hayward."

Simeon Hale quickly walked away, and Ann stood there helplessly, feeling sick and terrified. While she'd been warned about him, she'd not guessed there would be a confrontation between them. What he said was a direct threat against her. He was planning on harming her in some way, to revenge himself on John.

A minute later, William Collins came up to her. "Was Simeon Hale bothering you?"

She nodded. "Yes."

"I saw him here beside you and I knew it could mean no good," he said angrily. "I wonder how he knew who you were."

"I don't know," she lied, remembering that Eric had bragged about telling the musician who she was, in order to start just such a scene.

"The police should speak to Hale and prevent him from misbehaving as he does. What did he say to you?"

Ann, still in a fog of misery, turned despairing eyes to the old man. "He asked me what it was like to be the wife of a murderer!"

"The scoundrel!"

"I told him he was mad, but he went on."

"I know," William Collins said unhappily. "He's been talking that wild way ever since Susan was drowned. He can't accept the fact it was an accident. He still blames John."

"I'd like to get away from here," she said.

"Of course. Forgive me for not realizing that," William Collins said kindly. "Eric is remaining in the village for a while so we'll be returning by ourselves. Dawson is waiting for us."

He escorted her to the touring car and within a short time they were heading back towards Collinwood. No matter how dreadful her experience had been, Ann couldn't help congratulating herself on the fact she'd not allowed John to go to the affair.

It was late afternoon when they finally arrived home. "Would John like to come down and join me in a drink?" Collins asked as they entered the mansion.

"I'll ask him," she said. "That is, if he hasn't gone for a walk. I suggested that he should."

"I'll be in the living room," her host told her. "And if I were you, I wouldn't mention that meeting with Simeon Hale to him."

Ann nodded. "I'm sure your advice is good."

"It would only upset him and accomplish nothing," the old man went on.

"I agree," Ann said.

On her way upstairs, she met the housekeeper coming down. "Have you seen my husband?" She asked.

"Just a moment ago," the woman said. "He was standing in the hallway on the third floor."

"Oh?" she said. "I thought he might have gone out for a stroll."

"No, Mrs. Hayward. He's upstairs."

"I'd better go to him," she said, at once slightly upset. She couldn't imagine why John would be on the third floor and worried that his dark mood might have degenerated into a suicidal one. She was afraid he might be on his way to the rooftop of the house to make an attempt to take his life.

She quickly hurried up to the third floor and checked both

corridors. There wasn't a sign of John or anyone else. The house was deathly silent in the orange glow of the sinking sun. Deciding he must have returned to their suite, Ann went on back to the second floor and opened the door to their rooms. He wasn't there either, and true panic seized her as she decided she'd made a fatal error. She should have gone on up to the attic before returning to the suite.

She headed back towards the stairs. William Collins was standing on the landing. He looked alarmed. He had realized she was badly upset about something—perhaps the housekeeper had told him about seeing John—and he had come to help her.

"What is it?" he asked.

She paused a moment. "It's John."

"What about him?"

"He's vanished!"

"That's impossible!"

"I think he may be in the attic, or may have made his way to the rooftop," she said, her voice trembling.

"Surely not," he protested.

"He has had suicidal moments before," Ann said.

"Let me go up there," William Collins said.

"No," she said. 'You might drive him on to do whatever it is he has in mind. It will be better for me to reason with him." She quickly dashed on upstairs, leaving the protesting and bewildered man on the landing alone.

She didn't bother to hesitate on the third landing but went on up to the attic. There, on the fourth floor, she hoped to discover her missing husband, and if not there, perhaps on the rooftop. There was a final steep flight of steps leading to the Captain's Walk. If she wasn't too late, he would surely be there.

She quickly checked the corridor on the left. It was empty!

Then she heard a door near the end of the corridor on her right close quickly. It sent a surge of hope through her. She ran down the long corridor in the direction from which the sound had come.

"John!" she called out his name.

There was no reply. She tried the door and the handle twisted easily. She opened it and moved slowly into its shadowed, musty interior. It was a big room and her eyes were not accustomed to the sudden change to near darkness. She moved in among trunks and heaps of stored goods.

"John!" she spoke his name softly.

She thought she saw him crouched behind an old trunk in the far corner. She took a quick step forward, but as she did, the door of the room was slammed closed, leaving her in complete darkness, listening to her heart beat and the sound of footsteps rapidly vanishing along the corridor.

CHAPTER 7

Ann cried out in alarm at being trapped in the dark, musty room with its ghostly array of storage. The memory of the figure crouched in the corner made her more uneasy. Who could it be if it had been John who had closed the door on her and run down the corridor? Breathing fast from her frightened state, she hastily began to move backward towards the door. She thought she heard a rustling sound from the corner, which made her more terrified. In her urgency to escape, she stumbled over a carton and hurt her shin so badly that she cried out in pain.

Then she was at the door, groping for the handle. It was not locked, and she pulled it open again so that some light showed in from the corridor. Ann stared into the room and saw that what she had taken to be a crouching figure was no more than a grotesque shadow. Having satisfied herself on this point, she could only conclude that it had been her husband who had shut the door on her.

This meant he was somewhere on the attic floor or had continued on to the roof. Her concern for John grew. She made her way down the corridor which was only a degree lighter than the dark storage rooms off it. There was an eerie something in the air that troubled her. She again had the feeling she was being observed by unfriendly eyes. That someone concealed from her was watching her closely.

She'd gone the length of both corridors and there was still

no hint of John, so she climbed the steep steps to the Captain's Walk, pushed open the heavy door at the top, and entered the cupola atop Collinwood. There by the railing, stood John, staring somberly out at the panoramic view of the bay and the village beyond.

Ann hurried to his side and said, "I've been looking for you."

He glanced at her. "I saw you drive back in the car with William Collins."

Her brow was furrowed. "Then why didn't you come down and meet me?"

His eyes had a dull look. "It was so pleasant up here," he said, and immediately, Ann feared he had lapsed into a vague mood.

"But I've been frantic about you!" her voice broke.

He stared at her. "Why?"

"I didn't know where you were. I thought something might have happened to you."

"I'm not a child," John said.

Ann gazed at him in silent despair for a moment. How could she cope with this, make him understand? "You know I always worry about you. And why did you close the door on me when I was searching for you in the attic storage room?" she said gently.

He looked blank. "When?"

"Just now. I suppose before you came up here."

"But I've been up here a long while," he protested. "I didn't close any door on you."

Ann was startled. "If it wasn't you, who could it have been? I heard footsteps in the corridor afterward."

"I haven't any idea," John said, still staring out at the bay as if the whole thing was unimportant.

Ann tried to make some sense out of it. If John had been up on the roof all the time, she'd been stalked in the attic by someone else. But who? The last person she'd spoken to was the elderly William Collins. He wanted to assist her, but he was hardly the kind of person to close a door on her and leave her in a dark storage room. Who, then?

She gave her attention to her husband again. "There are things going on here I don't understand," she said. "I have the feeling we may both be in danger. I think we were wrong in coming to Collinwood."

John turned to her with a melancholy smile. "I hardly expected you'd be the first to succumb to the Collinwood phantoms."

"I'm serious, John!"

"So am I," he said. "I thought you were adapting very well here. Your friendship with Barnabas alone should be enough to sustain you."

She frowned. "Why do you resent my friendship with Barnabas?"

Her husband shrugged. "Perhaps because I realize he might have been a better husband for you."

"It's you whom I love!"

He regarded her sadly. "Wouldn't pity be closer to it?"

She was hurt and startled by his statement. "That's a dreadful thing to say!"

But John was ready to discuss this touchy subject with the cold clarity of the near insane. "Think it over," he said. "You'd been working for months in those hospitals crowded with wounded young men. An unending line of pathetic figures on stretchers had passed before your eyes. And suddenly, you centered your attention on one of those examples of human wreckage and made it your own to care for and restore to health. It happened that you selected me." A growing bitterness had come into his tone.

Ann gazed into his tortured eyes with alarm. "You mustn't believe that!" she protested. "You mustn't ever think it!"

"But Barnabas represents someone entirely different to you," John went on. "He is handsome, understanding, and so perfect in nearly every way you can hardly think of him as an ordinary human." He paused significantly before he added, "And that is the catch. There is a more than an even chance he isn't a normal human being, but a vampire like the first Barnabas Collins."

"You're talking just as wildly about him as you have about me," she said unhappily. "I can only forgive you because you're ill."

"Understanding would be more valuable than forgiveness," her husband told her soberly.

"Let's not argue," she said, realizing in his present state it would be impossible to talk to him with any degree of success. "You shouldn't be up here alone."

"Why not?"

"You're in too morbid a mood, for one thing," she told him. "It isn't good for you to be by yourself too much."

John smiled faintly. "I think it is very good for me. It offers me a chance to think things out."

"The catch is you generally always come to wrong conclusions," she said. "Come on downstairs with me. William Collins has invited you for a late afternoon drink."

By stressing that the owner of Collinwood was downstairs waiting for him, she finally persuaded John to leave the Captain's Walk, but it was like trying to coax a child and she was glad that Dr. Stair was coming the next day. Perhaps he would have some suggestions as to what would be best for John.

The balance of the afternoon passed without any notable incident. At dinner, William Collins referred to his meeting with Warren Miller.

"This fellow with the black bandage on his face seems very familiar to me. I can't say why, unless we've met before."

Eric smiled at her across the table. "I'd say Ann was the person here who knows him best. Isn't that so?"

She blushed. "I've only met him twice. But we have talked quite a lot on both occasions. He's a very intelligent, pleasant person."

John listened somberly, then said to her, "The fact he is a disfigured war veteran would prejudice you in his favor. You are so sympathetic towards us."

Ann was quite embarrassed by John's seemingly crude remark, but she tried not to let it show. "I've never let my feelings in this regard influence me."

Eric eyed her mockingly. "I'd go along with that," he said. "It has never struck me that you have a tender heart."

"That's such a dubious compliment I hardly know whether to thank you or not," she told him.

William Collins cleared his throat. "I hope Warren Miller pays us a visit so I can talk to him more at length, and perhaps place him."

After dinner, they gathered in the living room, as was the custom in the old mansion. John was not in a mood for conversation and slumped into a chair by the fireplace, and paid no attention to them. Ann talked with William Collins and Eric, trying to keep them from noticing John's strange condition.

But William Collins had noted it and made no secret of the fact. "Your husband doesn't seem to be himself tonight. He's been acting very confused since our return this afternoon."

"I'm sorry," she apologized. "He's not at all well."

"Where upstairs did you find him?" the old man wanted to know.

"On the roof," she said. "But before that, something odd happened. Someone else was up there and they shut me up in a dark storage room. I had quite a time finding my way out."

William Collins frowned. "Someone else? Who?"

"That is what I'd like to know," she said. "That's why I mentioned it. I thought you might have an idea."

"I have none at all," Collins said quickly.

Eric had another of his mocking smiles for her. "Perhaps it was one of the Collinwood ghosts."

"Perhaps," she said. "But it's the living I fear most."

Eric said, "Would Simeon Hale be a good example?"

"Perhaps," she said, "but mostly the person who encouraged him to annoy me."

"Interesting," Eric said slyly, but he lost some of his brashness since he certainly knew she was referring to him.

William Collins said, "You had quite a discussion with Dr. Stair."

"Yes. He'll be calling on John tomorrow. And I'm glad."

"Fine old doctor," he said with a nod. "I don't know what the community would do without him."

"Or without you, Father," Eric said, making obvious fun of his parent.

The old man looked annoyed. "It may suit you to make light of all the things I hold to be of value. But if you were suddenly removed from Collinsport, only your gambling cronies and the racetrack crowd would know you had gone."

"Which suits me perfectly," Eric said mockingly. "But I feel the talk has taken too serious a turn for our lovely guest. So I'm going to take Ann for a stroll in the garden."

Before she had a chance to protest, he'd taken her by the arm and led her outside. As they stepped into the pleasant dusk Ann said, "I didn't say I would go to the garden with you!"

Eric gave her a wink. "I was sure you would."

She studied the blond young man with wonderment. "You have more nerve than most people I've met. And you undoubtedly have intelligence. Why don't you try to make something of yourself?"

Eric smiled as they strolled along the gravel path of the rose garden. "Our family already has more money than any of us need. My father is dedicated to the business and to the town. I'm dedicated to enjoying myself."

"Is that enough?" she asked.

He halted and gave her a sudden, serious, look. "It could be if I had someone like you to share everything with."

She reproved him. "You know I'm married."

"John is ill and not fit to be a husband to anyone. He's hardly likely to survive long, if I'm any judge. You should soon be an attractive widow."

Anger flamed in her eyes. "How dare you talk like that to me?"

"Because I face facts. You don't approve of honesty, do you?"

"I don't approve of brashness and underhand tricks," she told him, "and you're adept at both."

"It's not my fault I've fallen in love with you," Eric protested.

"You have no right to discuss your feelings and you wouldn't if you truly had any regard for me," she pointed out. "I say you're in love with only one person and that is yourself!"

"Let me prove how wrong you are," he said.

With that, he took her in his arms for a tight embrace and a fervent kiss. She fought at him with her fists and tried to end the kiss without any success. After an endless time, he let her go. Ann slapped him across the face. "How dare you!"

He stood there, staring at her angrily. "You may regret that," he said.

"I'll take that chance," she told him.

There were footsteps on the gravel behind her and she turned at once, relieved to see Barnabas standing there. Ann could tell by the stern expression on his face that he had been a witness to the incident.

"Barnabas! I'm so glad you're here!" she exclaimed.

"I wanted to talk to you," he said quietly. He gave Eric a scathing glance and added, "Alone."

Eric smiled scornfully. "I wouldn't think of coming between a mismatched pair like you." With a final derisive glance, he walked away.

Barnabas came closer to her. "That was too bad."

"You saw it all?"

"Yes."

"Eric is impossible," she said with disgust. "I'm so thankful that you arrived when you did. You got rid of him, even if he did manage to say something nasty in leaving."

Barnabas smiled. "It was a small price to pay for his absence. How has your day gone?"

"It's been a difficult one," she said, then told him all that had gone on. She went into detail about the hateful manner in which Simeon Hale had treated her.

Barnabas listened carefully. "We can blame Eric for telling that mad Simeon who you are."

"Eric did it deliberately."

"And Simeon actually made a threat on your life," Barnabas said. "If you stay here, you should inform the police."

Her eyes widened. "You honestly think he's dangerous? He struck me as someone who would talk a lot—and do nothing."

"That may be so," he said seriously. "But you never can be sure when such people will turn violent."

"I suppose not," she said. "When I came home I had another shock waiting for me. John was nowhere to be found." She related her frightening experience in the attic, ending with, "I can't imagine who could have trapped me in that dark room. John denies it was him."

"Why not Eric?"

"It might have been," she agreed, "but I'm not sure when he got back from the village."

"It seems the type of malicious prank you might expect from him," Barnabas said. "Let's walk a little distance toward the cliff. He could still be somewhere near here in the darkness, eavesdropping on us."

"I hadn't thought of that," she admitted.

They left the garden and walked in the direction of the ocean. When they were a reasonable distance from the big, dark mansion they halted. Ann took a deep breath of the tangy air and gazed up at the stars.

"This could be such a peaceful place, but it isn't," she sighed.

Barnabas smiled grimly. "No fault of nature. The place is perfect—just blame it on the people here."

"That's so true," she agreed, and then remembered to tell him, "I almost forgot. I met Warren Miller again today."

"Really? Where?" Barnabas seemed interested.

"On Widows' Hill. We had quite a long talk. I don't know why you distrust him so. William Collins came by and I introduced them. It's strange, but William Collins seems to think he's met him before."

"I don't find that strange."

"Why?"

Barnabas gave her a wise look. "Because William Collins has met him many times in the past."

"Are you sure of that?"

"Very sure," Barnabas said. "I think the time has come to prove it to you." He took something from an inner pocket and passed it to her. "You may find this gold penknife interesting. I found it on a path Warren Miller uses every day. And according to my servant Hare, the day after I found the knife, Miller spent hours along the path, searching for it."

She felt the slim object in her hand. "It must be of great value to him. Why didn't you return it?"

"I have reasons."

"Oh?"

"Yes," Barnabas said. He took a small box of matches from his pocket and struck one and held the flame above her hand. "Read what is engraved on the pen knife."

She studied the knife in the flickering glow of the match and had just time to read the fancy script spelling out the name Quentin Collins. She raised her eyes to Barnabas.

"Quentin Collins!" she gasped.

He nodded solemnly. "So now you know who Warren Miller really is."

"You're sure he's Quentin?"

"Beyond a doubt. He's hit on this bizarre disguise to return here without anyone being able to recognize him."

"Playing on our sympathies as a war victim," she said with dismay.

"Quentin will play any game that suits his purpose."

"And what is his purpose?"

"To return here and observe what is going on. To do as he pleases. He wouldn't dare to openly come back—not when most of the village believe he is a werewolf."

Ann gasped. "Then that weird creature I heard howling the other night in the garden could have been Quentin transformed."

Barnabas smiled grimly. "If you care to accept the werewolf theory. Otherwise it was a giant stray dog."

"Do you believe the werewolf theory?" Ann asked, studying him closely.

"I have travelled too far and seen too many things to ever deny the possibility of the supernatural. But werewolf or not, I can assure you that Quentin is a devious person."

"Shouldn't William Collins be warned?"

"By whom?" Barnabas asked. "Certainly not by me."

"Why not?"

"Because he wouldn't believe me. My cousins at Collinwood hold me in an equally low esteem with Quentin. They are liable to be more worried about me than him. If I suggested he was in the area as Warren Miller, they'd think I'd made up the story to divert attention from myself."

She listened with dismay. "You believe that?"

"I know it. William Collins would never accept my word that Miller is Quentin. By the time they made a check, Quentin would be alerted and would be safely on his way."

"So you plan to let him carry on his charade?"

"Yes. We'll watch him closely and try to predict what he is up to. The chances are he just wants to enjoy the atmosphere of the village for a little. When he's had enough of home, he'll vanish one night."

"You sound very sure of that."

"It has happened before," Barnabas said. "I hope Quentin hasn't become romantically interested in you, too. He has been known to become obsessed with a pretty face and go to any lengths to capture it."

Ann said, "You make him sound frightening."

"I think it fair to say he is just that," Barnabas said. "So now you know why I asked you not to become too friendly with him."

"I wish you'd told me who he was at the start."

"It's a tricky situation," Barnabas said. "And I wanted to be sure I could trust you before I explained."

She smiled ruefully. "Which means I'm now on your trusted list?"

"You are."

"I suppose I should go in," she said. "John is very unwell. Dr. Stair is coming to see him tomorrow."

"I know Stair," Barnabas said. "He's a competent doctor."

"Everyone but Eric seems to think so," she said with some bitterness.

"You can discount what Eric says on most anything," Barnabas reminded her with a hint of disgust in his tone.

"It's strange," Ann said. "But the person John seems most jealous of is you. Whenever we have a quarrel, your name is always dragged into it."

Barnabas looked grimly amused. "I'm both pleased and sorry."

She sighed. "I'm sure it's because he knows I rely on you more than anyone else here."

"I'm proud of that," Barnabas said.

"He puts it down to both of us being English," she said. "Yet he knows it is more than that. Of course, he enjoys taunting me about the fact you've had troubles here."

There was a knowing gleam in Barnabas' eyes. "He undoubtedly has repeated the vampire rumors."

"Yes."

"One pays for being an individual in a small place like this," Barnabas said casually. "I prefer to work in the daylight hours and roam the countryside at night. My research sometimes takes me to the cemetery in the midnight quiet and often I walk alone on the village streets. The people here don't understand this so they had to find a tag for me."

She nodded. "And they remembered the rumors about your ancestor."

"Exactly," Barnabas said. "And so I at once became suspected of being the reincarnation of the monster!"

"I see you as no monster," Ann said impetuously. "You are a fine person."

"Thank you," he said gently. "I shall try never to do anything to have you change that opinion."

"Nothing would make me do so," she said.

He bent near her and touched his lips lightly to her forehead. Ann was astounded by the icy coldness of his lips. Then his deep-set brown eyes met hers in a gentle look. "I won't pretend that if circumstances were different I couldn't fall in love with you, Ann," he said tenderly.

"And I'm deeply fond of you, Barnabas," she replied in a near whisper.

He was holding her hands in his now and his glance didn't falter as he continued, "But since you are married and I am a lonely wanderer we must accept things as they are. I shall always be a little in love with you, but I'll never attempt to come between you and John."

"I know that," she said.

"No matter what anyone may tell you about me, take it with a grain of salt," Barnabas went on. "I'm not nearly as dangerous a fellow as they would make out."

"I'm sure you're not."

"I have the impression there may be serious danger lurking for you at Collinwood. Perhaps it would be best if you left there as soon as possible."

"That has been on my mind," she told him. "But John is so unwell I don't know whether it is wise to move him. I'll talk to Dr. Stair about it tomorrow."

"Do that," Barnabas urged, "and be careful where Eric is concerned. That young man has dangerous possibilities."

"I realize that," she agreed.

"I'll see you safely to the door," Barnabas said and they walked back in silence.

As she entered the house, Ann glanced back to see his tall, broad-shouldered figure vanishing in the darkness. Whenever she saw him leave her, she experienced the same feeling of desolation. A wave of guilt shot through her. Was John right? Had she fallen in love with him? Or had she turned to Barnabas merely because of the terrifying plight in which she found herself?

She went directly up the broad, dimly-lighted stairway to the second floor and along the shadowed hallway in the direction of her suite. Just as she was about to open the door, she saw a figure coming down the corridor towards her. It was Eric!

She didn't want another scene with the brash young man, so she quickly let herself into her room and bolted the door after her. Then she stood for a moment, listening. She heard him walk close to the door, and he actually had enough nerve to turn the handle. She watched with frightened eyes as he strained to open the door. Then there was a moment of silence and she heard his footsteps retreating.

With a deep-sigh of relief, she turned her attention to her own room and that of her husband. Everything was very quiet. She moved across to the open doorway and then received another shock at seeing that John's bed was empty.

It was obvious it had not been slept in and she glanced around the room to see if there was any clue to where he might be. She noticed that the door to the walk-in closet had been left open. Going to it, she peered inside.

The big closet was deeply shadowed, but not to the extent that she couldn't see that a door on the far wall was open. Her heart gave a leap! Apparently, John had gone through it to explore the hidden areas of the old house.

She was caught between a desire to call on William Collins for help or merely follow her husband and get him back to the safety of his room. He was in no fit condition to wander through secret passages. She stood there, debating what she should do. The memory of Eric stalking her in the corridor decided her. Better to try to find John on her own.

She went quickly back to her own room and found a candle in a holder. It took her a few seconds to light it and then she returned to the closet. She made her way cautiously through the secret door and found herself in a damp brick passageway with a circular, narrow flight of stairs that seemed to lead to the cellars. Candle nervously in hand, she began her descent.

CHAPTER 8

The passageway was damp and smelled of being closed a long time. Ann reached out and touched the wall with her fingers to balance herself as she went down the steep circular stairway, and the unexpected cold and wet of the wall made her cringe. Had John managed to get safely down here in the darkness? She continued on down the narrow stone steps cautiously—they seemed almost as slippery as the walls.

The steps kept winding down into the black silence and she was sure she was descending to the lowest level of the old mansion. At last she reached an earthen floor. She seemed to be in a long cellar with huge wooden support posts at intervals. The stale, earthy odor here choked her, and as there seemed to be nothing in the way of storage in the particular underground corner in which she had arrived, she was certain she could find John quickly and return upstairs.

The candle was of little use for illumination in such a large place. Its glow reached a very limited area. Ann stared into the shadows, searching for some sign of her missing husband, but there was none. Nor did she hear any intruding sound. She moved forward slowly, keeping in mind the direction from which she'd come so she'd be able to find her way back.

The collected dust and cobwebs gave the dank cellar more

than a suggestion of a century of abandonment. She began to worry that it might be infested with rats and stared down anxiously at the hard earthen floor, relieved to find no sign of rodents as yet. At last she came to what appeared to be a wooden dividing wall. There was a rough door almost directly in front of her and the fact it was partly ajar suggested that John might have used it. Hesitantly, she pulled it all the way open. Then, thrusting the candle before her, she surveyed the room on the other side of the doorway.

This room definitely was a storage section. It had a rough plank floor and walls of broad boards with spaces in between. Ancient trunks and wooden boxes were piled in every corner. There were also huge bundles of newspapers and magazines. Discarded furniture also had a place in the weird collection of cast-offs, which probably dated back more than a century. She moved around the stacks of dubious treasures, searching between columns of trunks and crates for John, finding not a trace of him in the cluttered room.

She was held back by the limited range of the candle's glow by which she could only examine a small area at a time. Slowly, thoroughly, she weaved her way through broken chairs, bed frames and battered tables to a far corner of the room—and then she saw it!

Ann gasped in horror! Neatly set out in this particular corner was a plain gray coffin. Its lid had been removed and the quilted white lining could be seen. The sight of it brought an eerie fear to her but she could not resist going closer to discover if there was anyone in it.

Her hand trembled as she held the candle higher and stared at the empty coffin. What was it doing here? Had some far-sighted Collins purchased it to use when the appointed time came, and then his survivors forgot about it?

Suddenly, she heard the faint movement behind her. It made her blood go cold and she listened in fear, waiting for it to be repeated. Then a board creaked to her right.

She wheeled around toward the sound, but the flickering glow of the candle revealed nothing. Ann was filled with the ominous certainty she was no longer alone. She was afraid to move, terrified that someone would suddenly spring at her, and pretended a nonchalance which she didn't feel.

Apprehensively, she backed towards the coffin and as she did, her foot bumped its side. She whirled around and stared down into the yawning casket.

Ann heard the pounding of her heart, and the sound made her realize she had been wrong in venturing down into this remote place alone. Anything could happen to her and no one would know. It would merely be a matter of closing the secret door in the closet, and she and John would have both vanished without a trace! She would have to admit defeat and find her way back—if she could find her way back.

As she turned and headed around a corner of some stacked trunks, she heard an odd choking sound, like a gasp for breath, from behind her. Before she could even react, the candle and candleholder were swept from her hand. She screamed in terror and plunged ahead, but not soon enough!

Strong hands seized her and dragged her back across the room to the area where she'd seen the coffin. She fought and cried out against her attacker but it did no good at all. She could not tell who or what it was that had taken hold of her, but she knew it was a force she could not fight. All at once, she was literally lifted from her feet and then, just as suddenly, thrown down again.

She was being forced into some kind of a small space. She kicked and tried to save herself without avail as her feet and legs were confined. She could only move within a limited area: her attacker had thrust her into some kind of box! Even as this thought flashed through her terror-stricken mind, a heavy covering was pushed down on her. Her hands felt cloth and now she had no real room to move her arms. She was completely helpless as she sobbed and tried to press up against this covering over her! And then she knew... knew that she was a prisoner in the coffin she had just seen!

It was becoming warm in the small space and the air was fetid. Ann felt that she would soon not be able to breathe. Perspiration poured from her in her panic as she continued to scream and pound against the lid of the coffin, even though she knew the chances of her being heard were small indeed.

Then weakness swept through her slim body and she lay gasping for breath for a minute, but the urge to survive was great. She began to search the covering of the casket for the place where the two sections met. She had a feeling that she might somehow find a means of raising the top if she could search out that seam. It gave her an immediate task. Perhaps it saved her sanity.

The quilted lining of the coffin was full of tucks which made it more difficult to locate the crack. She hunched her body down as far as she could and discovered that the lining only went partway down the length of the coffin. She found where it began and roughly ripped it up towards her. However, this created new problems and as the bulk of cloth gathered around her to combine with the dwindling air supply, she felt certain she was on the edge of suffocation.

She was still sobbing but she forced herself to keep working at this task. She had gained at least a limited control over her panic and she was battling to survive. Now, she could clearly trace the seam where the wood joined and she continued to feel for some weak spot, some place where she could lever the covering and escape from the fetid confines of the casket.

Knowing well the area in which she must work, she squirmed to the head of the casket so that most of her body was in that section. She positioned herself as well as she could in the limited space and braced herself against the covering in a mighty bid for freedom. Her shoulder hit the solid lid and she cried out from the impact. She dropped back with a groan. Then painfully, she began to turn in the dark, stifling area until she was on her other side. Again she braced herself for an escape attempt, but as she did, she was sure she heard someone moving around outside the coflin.

Ann began shouting and pounding again, and kept it up continuously, at least for what seemed to her to be minutes, then fell back gasping, exhausted. Nothing had happened! She was sticky with sweat and her head was pounding and a new fear began to creep into her mind.

Suppose she fainted and never became conscious again? She might just lie there, motionless until death arrived. This casket would then truly be a suitable resting place for her! It could happen!

The ache in her head and a sensation of growing weakness warned her that she had come close to the limit of her endurance. Her last wild outburst, her desperate screaming for help, had hastened her collapse. She had futilely expended valuable energy and now she was struggling for breath, hoping to conserve her precious strength as she fought the curtain of darkness which threatened her. The main thing was to keep her mental faculties clear. She knew that once she lost her grip on them she would be as good as dead.

Ann opened her eyes wide and stared into the blackness of the casket. So this was what it felt like to be buried alive! To gradually lose consciousness and then die alone and forgotten. She couldn't accept that! She had to make at least one more try, but what if the monster who had consigned her to this fate was waiting for her to escape? She didn't dare let that awful possibility linger in her mind. Instead, she braced herself again to use all her remaining strength to escape from the box of death!

Then a miracle happened! A faint scraping sound came to her ears and she realized the casket was being opened. Seconds later, the cover was lifted away and Ann immediately took several deep breaths of the cellar air which now seemed country-fresh. Only then did she see who her rescuer was—William Collins!

The old man held a lantern in his hand and he bent over her anxiously. "Are you all right?"

"I think so," she managed weakly as she saw a stunned-looking John standing behind him.

"I thought I heard sounds from this corner," William Collins went on, "but I couldn't believe there could be anyone in the casket.

Just as I was about to turn away, I heard your screams."

John helped her out of the casket. "I knew you must have come down here."

Ann stood shakily and leaned on her husband. "I came down after you," she said in a strained voice. "When I entered our rooms, I found a secret door open in the closet. . . and you missing."

John's hollow-eyed face showed remorse. "I did come down here," he was ready to admit. "The door had been left open before I went up to the bedroom for the night. I don't know who did it. We must have missed each other down here."

William Collins held the lantern up to examine her more closely. "You look dreadful. We must get you upstairs as soon as possible."

"I'll manage," she said in a shaky voice. "How did you know I was down here?"

"When John went back upstairs and found you missing he became upset. He decided, quite rightly, that you had followed him here to the cellars and might have gotten lost. He asked for my help."

"I see," she said.

"But that doesn't explain how you came to be locked in the casket," the squire of Collinwood said. "What took place down here?"

"I heard someone behind me when I was searching for John."

"Did you see who it was?" Collins wanted to know.

She shook her head. "I just heard this strange choking gasp. Then the candle I was carrying was knocked out of my hand and I was attacked."

"And your attacker actually put you in that coffin?"

"Yes. I didn't know where I was for a moment or two. It was all so confusing and it happened so fast."

John was trembling and again Ann felt a wave of pity and some alarm. He said, "It was my fault. I should have waited until you came to the room. I shouldn't have ventured down here on my own."

"There's no need to try and portion out blame now," she told him. "I had a chance to ask Mr. Collins for help without my coming here alone."

William Collins blinked unhappily. "I certainly wish you had called on me. It seems we have a would-be murderer in the house— an intruder, no doubt. Perhaps it was someone bent on theft whom you caught in the act."

"Perhaps," she said, but she was not in a fit state to discuss it at the moment. She still couldn't forget that it was Eric who had first frightened her in the corridor. That had been her reason for not asking his father for assistance. She'd been afraid of venturing into the hall—and so she had come to a worse fate.

William Collins asked, "Do you feel strong enough to go back upstairs?"

"I think so," she said.

"We don't have to use the secret passage," he said. "The steps there are much too steep and in any case, I've closed off that door. We'll go into the main cellar and use the regular cellar steps."

When they reached the main floor, William Collins put aside the lantern and took them into the living room. John led her to a divan as Mr. Collins went to the sideboard to prepare her a drink.

Holding the snifter out to her, he said, "A brandy is the tonic needed in a case such as yours."

She took a few sips of the amber liquid. It burned her throat but gave her a warm, comfortable feeling. William Collins stood by watching her.

"Is that helping?" he asked.

"A great deal," she said, taking another sip.

"I'd say you needed a drink, too," Collins said to John and returned to the sideboard.

John gave Ann a frightened look. "I can't bear to think of what might have happened to you down there. Who would do such a terrible thing?"

"I haven't decided," she told him.

John clenched his fists. "I'd like to get my hands on him!"

William Collins returned with a drink for John and one for himself and said, "I can't tell you what a shock this has been for me. The idea of one of my guests being attacked like this creates a most embarrassing situation."

"You mustn't blame yourself," she said, feeling better for the brandy.

"But it did happen here at Collinwood. Here in my house!"

She said, "I doubt that whoever was responsible is still here."

"First thing in the morning we must discuss this and decide what to do," Collins insisted.

"Yes," she agreed as she got to her feet. "I feel well enough to go on to my room now."

"I'll see you directly after breakfast," William Collins promised.

They said their goodnights and John escorted her up the stairs. She still felt weak and ill but she knew she had suffered no lasting injuries from her ordeal, except for the fear that would always remain with her.

When they reached their room, Ann checked and saw that the secret door had been closed. If she hadn't known it was there she wouldn't have noticed it. She came out of the walk-in closet and joined her husband.

"It's sealed off now," she said. "I guess we can forget it for the night."

He was staring at her fixedly. "It was my fault."

"No."

"It was," he persisted. "I found that door open and started down the stairs. Then I had some sort of blackout. It must have lasted for ages. I didn't come out of it until I was here in the room again. Then I went and roused Mr. Collins."

She listened with a new chill of fear going through her. She asked, "Did you see anything of Eric?"

"No," he said. "That is odd. Where was he that he missed all the excitement?"

"A good question," she said dryly. She was thinking what she would tell Eric's father in the morning.

Ann spent a dreamless night and awoke to another fine June day, feeling little the worse for her experience, except for a sore shoulder. John's condition was not as satisfactory. He still seemed in a kind of daze, as if he'd not fully come out of the blackout which he'd complained of the previous night.

When they finished breakfast, she urged him to go sit in the garden for a little. She promised to join him shortly. After he'd reluctantly gone out, she went down to the study for her discussion with her host. Again, she felt it odd that there had been no sign of Eric after the night of crisis.

William Collins was at his desk when she entered the study. He rose, waved her to a chair close by him, and went over and shut the door to give them privacy.

Offering her a rare smile, he said, "I'm delighted to see that you look very well this morning."

"I don't feel too badly," she said quietly.

The stern-faced man sat down at his desk again and gazed across at her. "So now we must decide about last night."

"Yes."

"Do you have any idea who might be responsible?" he asked. "Anyone you suspect?"

She hesitated. "Yes," she finally said.

He showed surprise. "Indeed? Who?"

Ann looked at him earnestly. "I don't want to upset you because you've been so kind to us," she said. "But I can't conceal the truth. I suspect Eric."

William Collins paled as if she'd struck him in the face. He was silent a moment, then he rose and said, "I didn't expect to hear my son's name mentioned in connection with this."

"I wish I could have avoided it," she said.

He came around the desk to her. "Why do you accuse Eric?"

"Last night, on my way to our rooms, Eric followed me down

the corridor. I locked the door against him. He tried to force his way in. It's not the first time he has behaved in such a manner towards me."

"I'm shocked to hear that."

"It's true."

Collins sighed. "Eric has always been wild and reckless. Quite unlike his brother, Tom, who died. Tom was gentle and retiring. I had great hopes for both my sons. But now, Tom is lost to me forever, and Eric is gradually destroying himself with drink and gambling."

Ann said, "He has many good qualities."

"I know," his father said. "That is what makes it so tragic. I'm still not agreeing that it was my son who made this attack on you. He might have followed you down the hall; that is possible. I doubt the rest—because of the simple fact I found him wandering around in the upper hallway, in a very drunken state, and helped him into bed."

She stared at him. "He was that drunk?"

"Yes," he admitted. "So I find it difficult to believe he was the one who trailed you down to the cellar and thrust you in that casket, unless he was drunk when he did it, and then returned to his bed. He was there when I went upstairs last night, and he is still sleeping off the effects of the liquor this morning."

This information left her confused. She thought Mr. Collins was speaking the truth, but if he was, then it couldn't have been Eric who attacked her, and his drunken condition gave him an alibi for his non-appearance last night and this morning. She swallowed hard. "I hope I haven't accused him unjustly," she said.

"I'm sure you wouldn't deliberately do that," William Collins said, studying her with his sharp eyes.

"No."

"And you are an intelligent girl."

"Eric has taunted me about various things," she said. "Perhaps because he has made a bad impression on me, I was quick to accuse him."

He nodded. "That's a fair explanation."

"I didn't see who it was."

"You had no glimpse of him at all?" Collins continued.

"No. The candle was knocked out of my hand. We struggled in the darkness."

"There was no sound of a voice?"

"No. Just a strange coughing sound before the attack on me."

William Collins pursed his thin lips. "It's a very difficult and unpleasant business. But I feel, knowing what you now do, that you wouldn't want to place any charge against my son."

"Not now," she agreed, though she still suspected that it had been Eric. She realized she could never convince this doting father of his son's guilt.

"So we must turn to other conjectures," William Collins said.

She stared up at him. "Yes?"

"I find myself in the same difficult position you were in a moment ago," he apologized.

Ann was puzzled by the subtle change in his manner. "In what regard?"

He went around and sat behind his desk once more. He clasped his hands in front of him and gazed at her soberly. "I think I know who your attacker was," he said.

Ann sat forward in her chair. She was beginning to feel the chill of the room's atmosphere—beginning to know what was in his mind.

She pretended ignorance. "Please go on," she begged.

"This is difficult after your ordeal last night."

"It has to be discussed. Who do you think attacked me?"

His sharp old eyes met hers. There was a long minute of silence. Then he said dryly, "Your husband."

"John!" It was her turn to be shocked.

"Yes."

"Why do you say that?"

He frowned. "Circumstantial evidence. But strong enough to make me believe he may be guilty."

Ann had known for some minutes that he was going to accuse John. Worst of all, she realized he might be correct; after all, she had thought of it herself.

She said, "Please explain."

"When he came to me for help your husband was very upset," the old man said.

"Finding me missing would upset him."

"I felt he was more shaken than he should have been," William Collins said. "He was trembling like a leaf. He could scarcely talk coherently."

"His shell shock has left him with spells like that," she said.

"I realize he is not mentally stable," Mr. Collins agreed. "But doesn't that make it seem all the more likely that he could have assaulted you during one of his mad interludes?"

She gave him a reproving look. "He suffers from blackouts, Mr. Collins, but he is not insane."

"I'm sorry if I phrased it too strongly," he apologized.

Yet all the while she was defending her husband, Ann was remembering: The first thing John had confessed when they were alone was that he'd had a blackout and he was blaming himself for all that had happened. He had been in a dreadful state—he still was, in fact.

"Is there anything else?" she questioned.

"Yes," he said. "When we went down to the cellar, he led me straight to where you were."

"So?"

"So it seems to me he must have known you were in that casket because he'd put you in it."

Ann knew the evidence was becoming stronger against John. It was really no surprise to her. She looked at the old man with weary eyes. "Did he take you to the casket?"

"No."

"So you can't truly say he led you to it."

"No," William Collins admitted. "But I do say he led me to the room where the coffin was and he seemed to know about it."

"I see," she said.

"When we heard the sound from the coffin he was very startled," he continued.

"That would be natural," she said. "It must have been an eerie experience for you also."

He sighed. "It was."

"I can't see why that should make John seem more guilty," she said.

"Perhaps I'm doing what you did earlier. Because I know of John's unstable mental condition, I can't see anyone else as guilty."

Ann sat in silence for a moment. "I can't deny the possibility that he is guilty."

"Can you think of anyone else who might have done such a terrible thing to you?"

"I can think of someone who would do it, given the chance—Simeon Hale."

He looked interested. "That is true. Simeon hates both John and you. And he threatened you only yesterday afternoon."

"If he could find his way in here, he might be guilty," she said.

"There are ways to enter this old house that can't be blocked off," he said. "Side doors and cellar entrances. I think he could get in here, if he wanted to badly enough."

"So we have at least one other suspect," Ann said. "Under the circumstances, with my husband possibly the culprit, I don't think the incident should be reported to the police."

William Collins looked relieved. "If that is your decision, I'll certainly go along with it."

CHAPTER 9

Ann's discussion with William Collins had been an unsettling one, and she excused herself from his study as quickly as she could. She made her way out of the house with a feeling of complete despair. The more she went over the possibilities, the more convinced she was that her husband was guilty of the insane attack against her. This time, he had acted out his nightmare in a different way.

In comparison with the evidence against John, Simeon Hale was a weak suspect. There was also still a possibility that Eric was the culprit. Even though, by his father's testimony, he was very drunk, he might have made it down to the cellars. Ann hadn't gotten a good enough look at him in the corridor to judge how drunk he was, but he had surely followed her and tried to get into her room.

Ann realized the evidence was overwhelmingly against John, and remembered all the grim opinions expressed by the hospital doctors when she'd married him. She'd done it against the advice of the best experts. For a time, she'd seen him justify her hopes by improving, but now it seemed to be all downhill. She was relieved that Dr. Stair was coming in the afternoon. Perhaps he might be able to help her unhappy husband.

Ann went outside through the sunroom on the left of the mansion, and found John seated at an umbrella table in the main garden. He was staring off blankly, as he so often did these days. He didn't even glance her way when she sat down beside him.

She put a hand on top of his. "A penny for your thoughts," she said.

He came out of his spell and gave her a hasty, rather frightened look. "I was thinking of back there. On a day like this... we'd been in the front lines for more than fifty hours, without relief. The sun was hot and bright as it is now, and then, suddenly, the battle broke. We saw them coming towards us over the barbed wire. And the shells began to roar!"

"You mustn't go over all that," she warned him. "The doctors told you it could harm you."

"I'm sorry," he apologized. "But it's so confused in my mind. It seems more real to me than my being here."

"It mustn't!"

"I know, but I can't escape it."

She said, "You may need some medical help. Dr. Stair is coming by to talk to you this afternoon."

John looked angry. "I don't need help. What can that old man do for me? You're wasting his time and mine."

"But you have time to spare these days. And after the doctor leaves, we can get a carriage from the stables and you can drive me in to see how the house is coming along. We've only been there once," she coaxed.

"I don't care about the house," he said, staring out across the garden again.

"But that is why we came back here—to have our house built and live in it."

"I don't think I want to stay in Collinsport," he argued.

"Why not?"

"I'm not happy here," he said.

"You're as happy as you're liable to be any place," Ann suggested. "Maybe you'd feel easier if we moved into the village and got away from this house. It has an ominous air about it, and after last night, I'd like nothing better than to leave."

John turned to her suddenly. His burning eyes mocked her. "Isn't that just a bit of acting on your part? Would you really be willing to leave Collinwood and Barnabas?"

She frowned. "Why must you bring Barnabas into everything?"

"Because you're in love with him!"

Ann stared at him with alarm. Surely there was madness registered on his gaunt face at this moment. "Why are you so unfair? Barnabas is merely a good friend."

"That's what you want me to believe," John said.

"You must believe it. You're living in a fantasy world.

Everything you imagine you decide must be true, and this leads to the blackouts such as you had last night."

He closed his eyes. "Don't remind me of last night."

"It was worse for me than for you," she told him. She decided it was the proper moment to see if she could learn anything else from him. "When you took William Collins to the cellar, why did you lead him directly to the room where I was?"

He hesitated. "I can't remember that I did."

"You must have. He says so."

John regarded her uneasily. "I don't know. I may have. I told you it's all mixed up in my mind."

"Did you lead him over to the coffin in which I was imprisoned?"

He stared at her. "The coffin?"

"Yes. You remember the coffin!"

"I think so," he faltered. "I can't be sure. I was standing there, and then he lifted up the lid and I saw you."

Ann was studying him closely. "Were you surprised?"

He shook his head. "No."

A sharp pang of horror shot through her. Controlling herself, she asked, "Why weren't you surprised?"

"Because I'd seen you in it before."

Tautly, she asked, "When?"

He looked at her in his despairing, bewildered manner. "In that nightmare. You always were in your coffin at the end. After I strangled you, I put you there."

Sick with horror, she said in a low voice, "And so last night, during your blackout, you attacked me and put me in that coffin!"

John shook his head. He was trembling. "No! No! I wouldn't do that to you!"

"You said you weren't surprised to discover me there!"

"But I didn't mean it that way," he protested. "I meant that I'm so mixed up all the time that it didn't strike me as unusual."

She sighed. "So you claim you didn't do it?"

"I didn't."

"But you can't remember anything that went on during your blackout?"

Fear showed on his emaciated face. "If I had tried to murder you, or did anything crazy like putting you in that coffin, I'd remember it!"

"Would you?" she asked wearily.

He nodded. "Yes."

"I wonder," she said. She didn't want him to see how hard it had hit her, so she got up quickly and walked away from the garden. She didn't stop until she was by the edge of the cliff. Then she stood staring out at the bay, with tears running down her cheeks.

The thing that crushed her was the feeling she had lost John and could no longer reach him. Most of what she said was lost on him. He was gradually retreating into his madness and soon he would live in a world apart from her, a tortured world she could not share, even though she loved him. He would have to be taken away from her, to some safe place, for his protection and hers. This was the way it had to end.

She stood there, lost in her reverie, for several minutes. Then she heard a horse coming toward her, its hooves pounding across the lawn, and a moment later, Eric swung out of the saddle of his spirited stallion and stood by her.

Eric held the bridle tightly and he smiled at her and said, "What's all this I hear about last night?"

"So you've finally shown yourself?" she said, dabbing away her tears.

"Sorry, I was a little under the weather. I didn't know a thing about what happened until a little while ago."

Ann studied him bitterly. "I'm sure you want me to believe that."

"It's true," he said. "And I want to help you. I honestly do."

"I'm not convinced."

"Do be," he urged her. "First thing, you'd better get rid of that crazy husband of yours before he finishes you."

Anger flared up in her. "How dare you say that?"

"Why pretend? We both know it's true. My father told me how he behaved last night. Who else would shove you in a coffin like that?"

"I don't want to discuss that or anything else with you!"

His smile mocked her. "Do you think Barnabas is a better prospect?"

"Let's leave Barnabas out of it!"

"I'll admit he's rich," Eric said. "Richer than I'll ever be. But there are some drawbacks. To be rich and handsome is good. To have a thirst for blood—young female blood—can be bad! Very bad!"

"Don't say such things about Barnabas!"

Eric laughed. "Ask Dr. Stair when he arrives. I understand he had to treat one of the village girls for shock late last night. She was found unconscious on the front street. She had a certain peculiar mark on her throat—a mark that might be traced to friend Barnabas."

"I don't want to hear about it!"

"You'll be hearing plenty about it," Eric assured her. "The last time a thing like that happened, my father ordered Barnabas to leave. Otherwise, he might have been run out of the village." With that final, biting comment, Eric mounted the nervous stallion again and rode off toward the stables.

Ann watched him ride away. She felt she had gone through as much as she could stand on this lovely morning. The phantoms of Collinwood had surely closed in on her. Not only was it likely that John was mad and had tried to murder her, but now she had learned that Barnabas was implicated in some dread scandal. Because Eric had suggested she query Dr. Stair about it, she had no doubt that it was true.

Ann still had faith in Barnabas. She was positive that whatever harm had been done to the girl had been the work of someone who had wanted to make it seem like Barnabas was involved. Who would be better equipped to do a thing like that than Quentin Collins? Quentin, the black sheep of the family, hated Barnabas, and would do him any harm he could.

But who else knew that Warren Miller was in reality Quentin Collins? She doubted that anyone did. Quentin was so well disguised as the disfigured war veteran that no one had recognized him and he was free to do all the mischief he liked. Ann had an impulse to rush into the old mansion and tell William Collins who Warren Miller really was. But would he believe her? And dare she do it without consent from Barnabas, who had warned her to keep the secret of Quentin's identity?

Tormented by these various predicaments, she waited for the doctor to come. He arrived, in his horse and buggy, early in the afternoon. By that time, the house had settled down to its usual quiet routine; William Collins had gone to his office in the village, Eric had ridden off somewhere, and John had complained of a headache and gone up to his room.

Ann was alone in the living room when the white-whiskered Dr. Stair entered the house. Before going up to John, she told him what had happened the night before.

The doctor listened with a serious expression. "I don't like the sound of it," he admitted. "The chances are that John put you in that coffin."

"I know," she said.

"If you find out for sure it was John, you'll have to make some serious decisions," he warned.

"I won't be able to let him stay on here."

"He will have to be committed," Dr. Stair said solemnly. "There is no point in bandying words. If the man is losing his mind, he should be put in a place where he can be kept under custody."

"It may not be that bad," she said, her eyes imploring him to give her some encouragement.

The doctor spread his hands in despair. "I hope it isn't, but the evidence is strong against him."

"Perhaps if you give him some sedatives..."

"We can try treatment," he sighed, "but I make no glowing promises. I've not had any shell shock patients before, but from what I've read in the medical journals, the serious cases never recover. As a nurse you surely know that."

"Yes," she said in a small voice.

"Weren't you warned against marrying him?"

"Yes."

"And you still went ahead with it?"

Her eyes met his. "I loved him. I still do."

"He's a lucky man," the doctor said with a sigh. "At least in respect to you. I'll do all I can for him." He glanced around uneasily. "Sometimes I feel this big mansion has a curse on it."

"Why do you say that?"

The doctor looked grim. "So much tragedy has been connected with its history. Even in the present, some dark things have happened. Take the death of Eric's twin brother, Tom, as an example. There was a fine young man, the opposite of Eric in every way."

"I've heard that before."

The doctor frowned. "Then one day after his return from college—he was a Yale man—he was stricken with some kind of disease. I tried to diagnose him and treat him, but he simply wasted away."

"His father sent him to Boston, didn't he?"

"Yes. We both felt some of the specialists there might save him, but nothing could help poor Tom. He died there."

"It must have been a dreadful shock for his father," she said.

"William has never been the same since. He reacted badly to Tom's death. Even had the boy buried in Boston, rather than bring him back here. I thought that was wrong and I told him so. And do you know what?"

"What?"

"William coldly turned his back on me," the old doctor said unhappily. "Just turned away from me without an answer. He had never done such a thing to me before, nor has he since. After that, he began to be more lenient with Eric. Up to that time, he'd practically disowned him, and Eric was living near Portland. But like the prodigal son, he came home, and all was forgiven. He's been doing pretty much as he pleases, ever since."

"His brother's death harmed him by giving him the upper hand over his father," she said.

"Exactly," he agreed. "I don't know what is going to come of it. And now Barnabas is in trouble again."

She was glad that Dr. Stair had brought this up, because it gave her a chance to question him. "What about Barnabas?"

He looked grim. "He bears another kind of Collins curse. Maybe you've heard about it."

"Only vague rumors."

"It began long ago when a Collins was forced to leave Collinsport because the villagers thought he was a vampire. A century has passed and the legend is still alive. Small villages are like that—they coddle their superstitions."

Ann stared at him with disbelief. "You surely don't believe such things as vampires exist today?"

"I don't," he said, "but the local people do."

"Haven't you tried to clear it up? To tell them they're wrong?"

He looked down at the carpet. "That is rather difficult," he said. "We're faced with a strange situation here. Last night, a young woman was attacked. She was found on a village sidewalk, in a dazed condition. On her throat was a mark similar to that which vampires are supposed to leave when they take blood from anyone."

"And they are blaming this on Barnabas?"

"There is a renewal of ugly talk," the old doctor said. "Barnabas has been accused of such things in the past. And the girl can't say who it was."

"But it's silly to put the blame on Barnabas simply because he has the same name as an ancestor who was linked with the vampire legend. Or is it because he is an individualist who likes to keep his own hours and dress as he pleases?"

Dr. Stair smiled ruefully. "There is more to it than that."

"What do you mean?"

"Barnabas has only himself to blame for the suspicions attached to him. He is, as you've said, an individualist. And that can be dangerous for anyone in a small village. Don't you agree?"

"To an extent. You can be criticized, but not hated—or feared."

"True. But Barnabas goes very far in his behavior, especially this thing about not showing himself in the daytime. His liking for midnight visits to cemeteries makes people look at him askance. They help perpetuate the vampire legend and he knows it, yet he flaunts these actions. And I think I know why."

"Why?"

"Because Barnabas is a harmless psychotic. But definitely a psychotic."

"That's impossible; he's a charming person."

"Many psychotics are."

"Please explain why you call Barnabas a psychotic."

"He behaves like someone tainted with the vampire curse.

And since I don't believe in the vampire curse, I can only assume that it is Barnabas who is the believer, and that he is acting out the role of his ancestor. It is my private belief that he even goes so far as to make fake attacks on these excitable village girls, in which he uses some instrument to gently puncture their throats to simulate the vampire teeth marks."

She listened incredulously. "You're saying that he enjoys playing the role of a vampire, and making people fear and hate him?"

"Yes," the doctor agreed. "I have to either settle for that, or admit he is actually a vampire, and I can't do that."

"Will this present scare last long?"

"It depends," he answered. "It will, if there are any more victims."

"And then what?"

"I'd imagine William Collins will order Barnabas to leave here. He did that two or three years ago. This is the first time Barnabas has been back since."

Ann listened, but she was thinking of Quentin. She blamed him for the attacks. She said, "Why couldn't it be someone else, trying to put the blame on Barnabas?"

"That's possible," he said. "But who?"

"Why not Quentin? Everyone agrees he is an evil person."

The doctor picked up his medical bag and stood up. "You're talking about another mad Collins now," he said. "He thought he could turn himself into a werewolf. Had a lot of people believing it, too."

"Quentin may be back again, causing trouble," she said.

"I doubt that. He hasn't been here in years. He wouldn't dare show his face in the village."

"I know that," she said quietly, thinking of the black bandage that covered half of Warren Miller's face.

"Now that we've settled all those things, we can go up and see what we can do to help John," he said pleasantly.

Ann was relieved to find John in a good mood. He gave the doctor a friendly greeting, and when he questioned him about his blackouts and hallucinations, he answered carefully and calmly. Ann was surprised and encouraged by his rational behavior, in contrast to his confusion of the morning and the night before.

Dr. Stair eyed John sharply. "We must attempt to get rid of the nightmares that are plaguing you."

John smiled. "I wish you could."

"We'll try some sleeping tablets," the doctor said. "Start with a mild dose, and work up gradually if you don't get any relief."

John laughed. "That sounds as if they're bound to go eventually, as soon as the medicine is strong enough."

"That's the theory," the doctor said.

"I have a different one," John told him.

"Oh?" the doctor glanced at Ann as he waited for her husband to answer.

"I think the ghosts of Collinwood have gotten into my brain," John said too brightly. "The place is filled with evil spirits, you know."

"That kind of talk has been going on a long while," the doctor said, closing his little black bag.

"There are things happening here that can't be explained," John insisted. "Things I've seen myself."

The doctor stood up. "I'd still like to try the medicine."

"Sure, Doctor," John said. "Let Ann supervise the doses. She's a nurse, you know."

"So I understand," Dr. Stair said. "You're lucky to have her."

Ann saw the doctor to the door. As he stood there a moment before leaving, he told her, "So far, I haven't been able to make up my mind about John."

"He can confuse you."

"In the beginning he was extremely rational," Dr. Stair went on. "Before I left, he displayed several symptoms of madness. I think we must keep a close watch on him. I'll send the medicine to you and come back again in a few days to observe how it has worked."

"Thank you, Doctor," she said sincerely.

He eyed her earnestly. "Be cautious. I sensed a hostility towards you in him."

"He's really very fond of me."

"The John Hayward you married was," he said soberly. "But I don't think he is the same John Hayward who is sitting alone in that room up there now."

Ann's face shadowed. "I'll remember. Thank you again."

She stood on the steps until the doctor drove away, then went back into the cool, shadowed hallway. She was upset. John hadn't been given a clean bill of health, although the medicine could help, and with luck, everything might turn out all right.

The doctor's talk about Barnabas had not been too encouraging, either. If the stories she'd heard were true, then things were far from easy in the village. It seemed clear enough to her that Quentin was maliciously trying to drag his British cousin's name into a scandal once again.

Ann hoped that John was feeling well enough to drive over to their new home. She went upstairs again, to ask him, before ordering a carriage. When she opened the door, she found him standing by the window, staring down at the garden.

"Well, the doctor was most hopeful," she told him, crossing to where he stood.

He turned to her and she saw the mad light in his hollow, burning eyes. "You think so?"

"Yes."

"I can't agree," John said. "I know he's playing a silly game with me."

"How can you say that?"

His thin face showed derision. "I behaved perfectly, to see how he'd react."

Ann felt a great sadness surge through her as she stared at the wreckage of the man she loved. "You made a good impression on him."

"I intended to. I wanted him to think I was stupid."

"But you aren't stupid!" she protested.

His mad eyes met hers. "He thinks so, and so do you. While he gives me sleeping potions, you plan to be with Barnabas!"

"Oh, no!" she protested. "We're not back to that again."

John stared at her with hatred. "I have never left it. I know why you brought me to this place!"

"It was you who brought me here!"

"You pretended that's the way it was," he said. "But now I know better."

"Please stop this silly talk and let us go see how the house is coming along," she suggested.

"I don't want the house finished," he said.

"You can't mean that!"

"I do," he said grimly. "I'm sending them orders to cease construction. I'll never live in this place where you've disgraced me."

"John, please!" she begged.

His voice was full of hatred. "I'm weary," he said. "I want to rest. I wish you'd go and leave me in peace."

"Very well," she said. "I'll go. I hope you're better when I come back." He didn't answer, and after a moment, she went to the door and left.

Her throat was tight with hurt. She could only pray that the doctor's medications would help her husband, and bring him back to some semblance of normalcy. She could not bear to see and hear him acting in this manner. He was like a different person.

Ann slowly made her way downstairs. She didn't want to go to the construction site alone, and decided to forget that idea until John had improved. And if he didn't improve, she hardly knew what she'd do. She wanted to talk to Barnabas about it when she saw him in the evening.

It was awkward that she was never able to contact him in the daytime. Surely, he could occasionally relax this rule, especially in the case of emergencies. But she knew that his burly servant, Hare, would be difficult to reason with.

On an impulse, she decided to walk over to the old house where Barnabas was staying. It would occupy some of her time. She wanted to forget her angry scene with John, and the fresh air and sunshine always helped. It was hard to remain moody on a pleasant afternoon.

It took her about ten minutes to reach the ancient, vine-covered, brick building which was known as the old house. The green shutters were closed so that it would seem it wasn't occupied. Another one of Barnabas's strange quirks. Perhaps Dr. Stair was right, and the man she admired so much was obsessed with the idea he had the vampire curse.

She was going to go up the steps and try the door, but at the last moment decided against it, knowing that Barnabas would probably not approve. So she strolled on by the dark, silent building and began walking down the broad field leading to the Collins family cemetery. She had always wanted to see it, and perhaps now would be as good a time as any.

There was a small breeze that made the trees which fringed the graveyard stir a little. They seemed to sigh. Ann heard this rather mournful sound as she hesitated at the open iron gates of the cemetery. Then, feeling a little awed by the array of gravestones, she went on inside. What she hadn't realized yet was that someone was following her.

CHAPTER 10

The Collins family cemetery! She hesitantly moved in among the neat green mounds of earth, each marking the resting place of some Collins, and studied the weathered gravestones that gave their owners some slim degree of immortality. It was a quiet, shadowy place with a number of ancient elms standing proudly among the granite forest of headstones and tombs. Their seemingly everlasting vitality contrasted with the drabness of the orderly array of headstones.

The place held a strange fascination for her, and she could understand why it attracted Barnabas, whose interests were those of a historian. This haven of the dead seemed as remote from Collinwood as the old mansion was from the village itself.

Ann moved slowly from grave to grave, was surprised to find that some of the thin, weathered stones went back for almost two centuries! Surely there was a wealth of history in the quaintly weathered scripts. When she came to a large tomb with the name of Josiah Collins on it, she made a note of it, intending to discuss some of the more imposing stones with Barnabas later.

In her absorption with the graveyard, she forgot her own troubles for a while. Without realizing it, she moved deeper and deeper into the cemetery. She was reading the marker of a teenage girl who had died of a fever in 1817, when she suddenly stiffened and a frown crossed her attractive face. For once again she had the sensation of malevolent eyes being fixed on her. . . of an unseen glance of hatred which she could actually feel!

She wheeled around suddenly and discovered Simeon Hale standing behind her. The musician was hatless and wearing a shabby black suit. He was watching her with a sneering expression on his long, narrow face.

"I didn't know you were standing there!" she exclaimed, too surprised thus far to feel any fear.

"I come here fairly often," he said.

She was troubled by his too-bright fanatical eyes. "I have never been here before," she said.

"Do you like it?"

"As much as any cemetery," she said. "To me, they are all tinged with a sadness. . . the final evidence that we are truly mortal. That all are evened here in this last resting place."

He smiled coldly. "I don't think that is quite true. The question of status is not even settled here. You will note that some of the gravestones and tombs are much more imposing than others."

"Does that have any significance?" she wondered.

"It is a last grasp for the values of society," Simeon observed bitterly. "But I agree that it is largely a futile one."

"It seems a rule that people only go to cemeteries when grief is fresh," Ann said. "After that, just the historians or those responsible for the care of the graves show any interest, so pomp in such a place is doomed from the start."

The cadaverous face of the musician showed cold approval. "For a young woman, you show a remarkable intelligence. What a pity you wasted it in marrying John Hayward."

Ann was at once on her guard. She wondered whether this madman had deliberately followed her to this lonely spot or whether he really did visit it regularly.

She said, "I'm not sure I understand you."

"I think you do," he said obscurely.

"You say you visit here often?" she questioned, for want of something better to say. Slowly, tension mounted in her as she realized she was alone with this strange man in a place isolated enough for him to make an attempt on her life if he wished.

Simeon Hale moved closer to her. "Yes. I come here regularly," he said grimly. "Unlike the people you mentioned a few minutes ago, my wounds of grief remain fresh."

"I question that attitude as bordering on the morbid," she said. "I have just returned from serving in the war. I saw death too often and in too great quantities to want to embrace it. Life is for the living. That is the way our faces must be turned."

"Even when the dead were the most important to us?"

"They live in our memories—not in cemeteries," Ann argued with him. She felt if she could keep him engaged in conversation, it would be better for her and she might get away from him safely.

"I feel the tug of the grave," Simeon told her icily.

"Memories are living," she said. "What you have here are mouldering flesh and bones."

A grim smile crossed his cadaverous face. "You interest me more and more. Again I say you are wasted as the wife of John Hayward."

"Why should you hate my husband so?"

"He was responsible for the death of my sister."

"That's not true. Your sister drowned accidentally. It happens to many people who are good swimmers."

"No," he said, with a shake of his head. "I understood Susan better than anyone. She was heartbroken and she wanted to die."

"If you'll consider all the facts fairly, you'll realize how wrong you are," Ann warned him.

"Did you know that Susan is buried here?" the musician asked.

"No. Isn't this for the Collins family only?"

Simeon Hale's smile was sinister. "It happens that on my mother's side we are related to the Collins family. So Susan had a right to rest here if she wished."

"I see," she said quietly.

"It was my request that brought her here," he went on fanatically. "She was young and lovely, and she brings a certain grace to this pleasant cemetery."

"If it gives you satisfaction, I'm sure you did the right thing," she said, wanting to humor him. She could tell it would take very little to send him into an uncontrollable rage.

His eyes met hers. "Let me take you to the grave," he said. Without waiting for her to consent, he took her by the arm and led her along a row of graves to a distant point in the cemetery.

His grip on her arm was insanely tight and Ann was more frightened than before. "I must be getting back to Collinwood. I'll be missed."

Simeon didn't appear to be listening to her. He said, "When you married John and came here, you risked the curse of the Hayward Brides—or haven't you heard the legend?"

"I've heard of it," she said in a small voice, "but I don't believe in such stories."

Simeon chuckled mirthlessly. "Perhaps you should have. Every time a Hayward has brought a bride back from outside the district, she has died in a tragic fashion. First there was Elvira

Hayward from Boston, 1802 to 1829. Elvira hung herself!"

Ann was cold from fear. "I'd rather not hear about them!"

"But you should," he insisted. "The next Hayward wife to die was Sabrina. She has a stone in the town cemetery, the dates are 1854 to 1877. Sabrina became mad and set fire to her room, burning herself to death!"

"Please," she begged, trying to draw free from his grip as he roughly led her to a remote part of the burial ground. "Let me go!"

"Not until I finish," Simeon Hale gloated. "The third Hayward wife from the outside to die miserably was Jennifer. Her dates were 1869 to 1907, so you see she's only been dead some dozen years. She was shot and killed by a jealous husband."

"None of it has anything to do with me," she protested, near tears.

"I differ with you on that," Simeon Hale said. "You are from outside and you are a Hayward wife. It is my belief history will repeat itself!"

They came to a modest grave set aside from the main area of the cemetery. A gray headstone with the head and shoulders of an angel towered over it. Susan Hale's name was engraved on it. There was more lettering, giving her birth and death dates, and a sentimental poem which was signed "your loving brother." It was a maudlin and unhappy tribute, clearly proving Simeon Hale's sick state of mind.

Simeon stared fixedly at the stone. "I am here, Susan," he said in a hushed voice.

Ann stared at him in alarm. He was more disturbed than she had guessed. "Thank you for showing me the grave. I must leave now."

Simeon still stared at the grave. "There lies the girl who should have been John Hayward's wife!"

"You mustn't brood about such things! No one can change the past!"

"You took the place that was rightfully hers!"

"I never even met your sister!" she protested.

"And so you should die as she died." He turned to her suddenly, and Ann gasped in horror as she saw the look in his eyes.

"That's a mad thing to say!"

He nodded slowly. "You should join her in sleep here," he said in an eerie voice.

"Please!" she begged, and began to struggle to free herself. "Let me go!" she screamed. He laughed maniacally and went on holding her arm.

In the midst of their struggle, something completely unexpected happened. A third person appeared and quickly came between Ann and the crazy musician, and then hurled Simeon Hale to the ground beside his sister's grave.

Her rescuer was none other than Quentin Collins or the disfigured veteran, Warren Miller as he wanted to be known. He gave her a hasty glance. "Don't be frightened," he advised her, and then turned disgustedly to the fallen Hale. "What exactly were you trying to do?"

"We were just talking," he said nervously as he cowered on the grass.

"You were holding this young woman here against her will!" Quentin accused.

"No," Hale protested, still on the ground.

Quentin regarded him with contempt. "I'll let you leave because I know you are not fully responsible. Get up and get out of this graveyard within the next couple of minutes or I may change my mind."

Simeon Hale had lost all his bravado. "I have no intention of remaining," he said, scrambling to his feet. And then, pointing a skinny finger at Ann, he added, "Don't believe anything she says. I was only showing her my sister's grave."

"Get out!" Quentin said sharply.

Simeon needed no further warning. He shuffled off and didn't look back once. In a few moments he was out of the cemetery and making his way up the sloping field.

Quentin turned to her, the black bandage still covering half his face, and said, "That could have turned into something nasty."

"I know," she said, a tremor in her voice.

"Why did you come here with him?"

"I didn't," she said. "I came here alone and he either followed me or found me here by accident."

"So that's how it happened," Quentin said grimly. "It should teach you not to come to isolated places like this by yourself."

"I hadn't realized there would be danger in day light."

"You do now," Quentin said.

"Yes," she said quietly. Her fear was leaving her and she was taking stock of her position. It was a weird twist of fate that had made Quentin her rescuer—Quentin whom she blamed for the harm done Barnabas, and whom she didn't want to be in debt to.

He studied her for a minute. "You don't seem exactly delighted to see me. I may have saved your life."

"Yes," she agreed. "Thank you."

The single eye that was uncovered had a shrewd gleam in it. "I'd say you have changed in the last few days."

"Perhaps I have."

"Why?"

"A great many things have happened," she said carefully.

"I warned you Collinwood is not a happy place."

"So you did," she said. "William Collins was interested in meeting you. He has an idea he had met you someplace before."

"Indeed?" There was a sharp edge to Quentin's voice.

"Do you think that is possible?" she asked, wanting to hear what he would say.

He was completely calm. "We may have met. I don't seem to recall him."

"You probably would, if the meeting had been recent," she said. "Perhaps he was wrong."

"That's very likely," Quentin said in a dry voice.

"But you should visit Collinwood and talk with him and Eric. I'm sure you'd find them interesting."

Quentin's lip curled. "I doubt that. In any case I expect to be leaving here shortly."

"So soon?"

"Yes."

"But you have met Barnabas Collins," she said, deliberately leading him on and trying to get some evidence from him that he was Quentin.

He frowned. "If you mean the man in the caped-coat, we have passed on the beach. We're not exactly friendly."

"But he knows about you," she protested. "And if I remember correctly, you are well-informed about him."

The uncovered portion of his face showed a cold expression. "Barnabas happens to be a widely-discussed person today. It seems he visited the village last night, and left some evidence of his visit."

She allowed her eyes to meet his. "You're talking about that girl, the one they found with a mark on her throat?"

"You know all about it?" he sounded surprised.

"Enough," she said.

"Then you should stay clear of Barnabas in the future, knowing what he is."

"I'm not convinced he's to blame for last night," she said, defending the man she'd come to admire so much.

Quentin chuckled mirthlessly. "That's an interesting thought. But I don't think even Barnabas would be able to help you prove it."

"It might be worth a try," she said. "Barnabas has enemies like everyone else."

"Granted."

Ann could tell that Quentin was on his guard and there were unlikely to be any admissions from him. It would be better to end their discussion at this point, so she said, "I must go back."

"I'll go with you," he said.

"Don't put yourself out," she protested. "I've been enough of a nuisance to you as it is."

"I'm glad to do it," Quentin told her. "I only happened to be passing by the cemetery when I heard you scream. I was on my way to the woods and the swamp beyond."

As they were walking out of the cemetery, Ann asked, "Is there a swamp beyond the woods?"

Quentin nodded. "Yes. When I was a boy I used to go there often. It's quite a fantastic place."

"I like swamps," she admitted. "There's something so brooding about them."

Quentin glanced at her. "Don't get any ideas about going there alone. It can be dangerous."

"I'll remember that."

"See that you do. The place is full of large ponds and around the edges of them, there are sections of quicksand. I've seen small animals vanish in that soft mud in a matter of minutes."

"Terrifying," she said.

"Years ago a couple of escaped convicts took refuge in the swamps," Quentin said grimly. "They were never seen alive again."

"You think they were swallowed up by the quicksand?"

"Yes. Of course, the incident started all sorts of wild rumors and added to the legend of Collinwood."

"I had no idea you were so familiar with the estate," she said, studying him closely. "You talk more like a Collins than a person who has merely been a visitor."

"Do I?"

"Yes."

He shrugged. "I guess I've taken a lot of interest in the village and Collinwood in particular. Eventually it does become very familiar to you."

"So you know all the legends associated with the mansion?"

"Most of them."

"What about Quentin Collins?" she said, staring at him again.

He halted suddenly and gave her an incredulous look. "Why do you bring up his name?"

Ann raised her eyebrows. "Must I have a special reason? I just happened to hear his name mentioned by William Collins."

"What did he say about him?"

"That you reminded him of Quentin," she said, thinking this might make him reveal himself.

But the man with the black mask was wary. "Not having seen Quentin, I wouldn't know. But from what I've heard, Quentin died years ago."

"I don't think so," she said. They say he can transform himself into a werewolf."

Quentin scowled. "That nonsense!"

"Don't you believe such things can happen?"

"Do you?"

"I'm no longer sure," she said, evading any direct answer. "But I have an idea William Collins does, though he claims to be a skeptic in such matters."

"I have never been interested in Quentin Collins," he said.

"That's odd. He's such a fascinating character."

He gave her a thin smile. "It was my impression you preferred Barnabas."

"I do like Barnabas," she admitted.

"Even after last night?"

"Even after last night."

They resumed their walk and soon came to the grim structure of Barnabas' house. There was still no sign of life around it. Quentin gave her a knowing glance.

"Barnabas is very particular not to be intruded on during the day. Hasn't that ever struck you as odd?"

"Not especially," she said.

"I'd think about it if I were you ," Quentin said.

"I consider Barnabas a dedicated man," she told him. "Probably a genius of sorts. You can't question genius." They walked on until they reached the front lawn of Collinwood.

Quentin told her, "I'll leave you here. It seems Simeon Hale didn't remain on the grounds."

"No. I'm sure you've given him a good scare. Perhaps he'll not bother me again."

"I hope not," Quentin said.

"Why not come into the house for a moment?" she invited. "Some of the family may be there. I'd like to report how courageous you were in coming to my aid."

"Your own thanks is quite sufficient," he said. "I'm still ill at ease in the presence of strangers."

"I hope that one day soon the surgeons will properly restore your face," she said, knowing that behind that black silk bandage there were no scars. That Quentin simply wore it to conceal his identity.

He accepted her statement soberly. "Thank you," he said. "If I don't see you again, it has been pleasant knowing you."

"Are you really thinking of leaving soon?"

"There are reasons why I must," he assured her.

She thought she knew what they were. He had an idea his disguise was in danger of being penetrated, and that at any minute he might be exposed as Quentin Collins. She had probably worried him with her reference to William Collins.

She said, "Thank you again. I'll watch for you on the beach."

"Do that," Quentin said.

She stood on the lawn alone for a few minutes after he'd headed in the direction of Widows' Hill. Then she turned and started towards the front entrance of Collinwood.

She'd only gone a few steps when she once more had the sensation of eyes upon her, of someone balefully studying her without her knowledge. A kind of glitter passed across the grass in front of her, and she automatically lifted her eyes to the rooftop of Collinwood and the Captain's Walk. A solitary figure was up there, holding a pair of field glasses on her.

The glint of the sun reflecting on the glasses had caught her attention. Now, she shadowed her eyes to see who it was. When the man on the Captain's Walk put down the glasses, she was barely able to make out his features. It was Eric Collins!

Eric must have realized she had recognized him, for he at once vanished. Ann walked on to the entrance to the old house, thinking how odd it was that Eric had been watching her and Quentin with the binoculars. What had he hoped to gain by spying on them? It was a reminder of what she faced in the old mansion.

John was sleeping in his room when she went upstairs, so she stretched out for a short nap on her own bed. Her meeting with Quentin had a dream-like quality, as did the unpleasant moments when Simeon Hale had threatened her life. She decided it would be best not to mention either of these things to the others at Collinwood. It would only disturb her husband.

Once this matter was settled in her mind, she closed her eyes and slipped into a light sleep. She slept for perhaps an hour. Then she opened her eyes suddenly to look up into her husband's thin, anxious face. John was standing at her bedside, staring down at her.

She gasped. "Have you been watching me while I was sleeping?"

"Yes," he said quietly.

Ann raised herself on an elbow with a weak smile. "You know that always wakes me."

"I'm sorry."

She studied his emaciated face and thought he looked better. "You seem to have benefited from your rest," she said.

"I feel better," he agreed. "My head has stopped aching and I seem to be able to think more clearly."

"Fine," she smiled.

He sat down on the side of the bed and took her hand. "I was hateful to you this morning, wasn't I? And when the doctor came, I was just as bad."

"It doesn't matter."

"It does to me," he told her urgently. "I don't want to do those things, but I can't seem to stop myself. It's as if I were two different people. I can stand outside myself and listen to what I'm saying, but I can't control myself."

Ann smiled at him tenderly. "You mustn't worry about it. You're the John I married now. And it's wonderful to have you yourself again. The doctor has sleeping potions for you and I'm sure we'll get your nerves back to normal."

He looked at her and sighed. "I don't deserve a wife like you, Ann. I never have." He bent close to her to gently give her a kiss.

She held him to her for a long moment. When they parted she smiled and said, "As soon as you're better we should leave Collinwood. I'm sure we'd be happier some place in the village. This house is too overwhelming, too large and grim!"

"Whatever you say," was her husband's reply.

Ann dressed for dinner feeling happier and more optimistic than she had for some time. The improvement in John's condition was notable, and though she knew it might not last, she was grateful for even a brief interlude of normalcy. It proved there was still hope for him.

She wore a yellow gown and John had changed to a dark blue suit. When they went downstairs, William Collins and his son, Eric, were having cocktails in the living room. She and John went in to join them. Eric at once moved away, supposedly to get drinks for them, but privately Ann thought he was embarrassed because she'd caught him spying on her with the binoculars.

William Collins smiled when he looked at John. "You're looking much better, young fellow," he said.

"I feel more myself," John said with quiet politeness.

Mr. Collins nodded. "Just a matter of enough of our good seaside air and you'll mend."

"That's what I've been telling him," Ann agreed.

Eric came with their drinks. "I've made the usual," he said. "Is that all right?"

"Yes," she said, taking hers from him and trying to catch his eyes, but he skillfully evaded her and turned to John and handed him his glass.

Eric told John, "There was a lot of excitement in the village today. And I hear the town constable is even planning to call on Barnabas this evening."

William Collins glanced at his son worriedly. "Is that really true?"

"It's what I heard," Eric said. "The constable knows there isn't any point in going to see Barnabas in the daytime—he's had an experience with Hare before. But he does plan to question Barnabas about the attack on the girl."

John looked startled. "I don't recall hearing about that."

"Probably because of your illness," William Collins said and moving over to John, he began to go into the details of the attack on the village girl.

This left Ann and Eric together. She took a sip of her drink and said, "I saw you watching me from the Captain's Walk through your binoculars."

He frowned. "What binoculars?"

"You know," she said. "I was with that Warren Miller and you were spying on us."

Eric's face crimsoned. "Oh, then? I just happened to be out there and you came along." But she could tell by his tone that this wasn't the truth!

CHAPTER 11

As darkness approached, Ann became more nervous. She sat with the others in the living room of Collinwood after dinner and wondered about Barnabas. She was anxious to talk to him and hear his version of what had happened. She also wanted to tell him what had taken place in the cemetery during the afternoon. Eric had said the town constable was paying Barnabas a visit to question him. She worried what the results of this might be.

While she waited, a carriage came to the door, and the housekeeper entered the living room and called her out. Dr. Stair was waiting in his carriage in the driveway, the maid told her. Ann went outside to him and he handed her the package containing the bottle of sleeping portion.

"I had to come out this way," he explained, "so I decided I would bring it myself."

"Wonderful," she said.

"We're going to have a thunderstorm," the doctor said, observing the eerie stillness in the air.

"It is a weird kind of night," she agreed.

"You can hear voices a half-mile or more," Dr. Stair said. "That's a sure sign there's a storm on the way."

"John seems much better," she said. "When I talked to him later this afternoon he was almost himself."

"You can expect these variances in behavior."

"I hope it's a good sign."

"It may very well be," the veteran doctor told her, "but don't count on it too much. I think John is a very sick young man."

"I know," she sighed.

"See that he takes that medicine and adjust the dose according to results," the doctor advised, then said goodnight and drove away.

John was standing in the reception hall waiting for her when Ann went back inside. There was a questioning look on his emaciated face. "Who was that?"

"Dr. Stair," she said. "He left your medicine."

John looked moody again. "I feel fine. I don't need it."

"He thinks you should take it."

"I will if my head begins to bother me again," John said. "Otherwise I don't want to take a lot of drugs I don't need."

Ann could see the danger signs in him. At this point, it wouldn't do to try and force him into taking the medicine. Best not to upset him now, and try and talk him into it later.

She said, "Do whatever you think best. I'll take it up to the room and leave it there."

She left him to go upstairs with the medicine. In the room, she went to the window and stared out at the dark night. From the stables she could hear the workers talking, their voices coming to her loudly through the screen. The doctor was right, there was bound to be a storm. And she hadn't heard from Barnabas yet!

When she returned downstairs she found the living room empty, save for William Collins, who was seated before the fireplace, smoking a cigar. She went to him quickly. "Where is John?"

"I can't say for sure. He went out somewhere."

Her tone was troubled. "You're sure?"

"Yes," he replied. "Anything wrong?"

"No," she said. "At least, not yet. I'd prefer that he didn't wander off alone at night."

"He may not have gone far," William Collins said. "He's probably out on the steps or standing on the lawn."

"I'll look there," she said as she left.

Eric had also vanished somewhere, but she hadn't asked about him. Now she hurried out to the darkness of the front steps. It was hot, oddly hot for that time of night. The stillness of the air was as noticeable as before, sounds carrying a great distance. Far out on the bay she saw the colored lights of some pleasure craft. She strained her eyes to see some sign of John on the lawn, but he wasn't there.

All at once a great flash of heat lightning lit up the sky. It lasted only a second before darkness returned once more, but it was a warning of what might come. She went down the front steps and over to the garden. Moving from one part of the hedged, flower-bedded area to another, she searched vainly for her missing husband.

There was no sign of him and now she became really worried, as she thought of the cliffs and John in such a melancholy mood. Swiftly she set out across the lawns to the cliff path. As she reached the edge of the cliffs, the lightning came again in a revealing flash. It faded again, leaving her in the almost jet blackness of the unusual night.

She could not see John anywhere. Then she began to wonder if he might have decided to go see Barnabas for some reason. Perhaps he had made a pilgrimage to the old house. This idea bore down on her so hard she changed her direction and went directly across the lawn again towards the house where Barnabas was living.

As she hurried along, a drop of rain hit her forehead. A moment later, the heat lightning flashed once more to eerily reveal the sprawling lines of Collinwood and all of its out-buildings. It faded and left her thinking of the war days in London, of how she used to look out on the city from the hospital roof, with its battery of anti-aircraft guns and search lights. She recalled the first time she'd seen the giant sausage-shaped form of a zeppelin float over the city. As the floodlights had caught it in their beam, the scene had been lit weirdly like the one revealed by the lightning now.

Life had moved so swiftly during the war years. Her life had changed so fast. Little had she expected then that just a few years later, she would be the war bride of a shell-shocked veteran in this isolated section of America, nor had she anticipated anything like the tension-filled period she'd known at Collinwood.

Now she was passing the stables and ahead on the left was the old house. How strangely dark it was! She had never seen the shutters removed from its windows, and so any light would not show outside, nor would any daylight enter those ancient rooms. Reaching the front steps of the house, she went up and knocked on the door.

Only a few seconds later the door was opened by Barnabas. She gave a small exclamation of relief on seeing him. "I was afraid I wouldn't be able to reach you," she said.

His handsome face showed a grim smile. "I'm very much available tonight. The town constable has just left after calling on me."

"I heard he was coming," she said as he showed her inside.

"Bad news travels fast." Barnabas led down a dark hall to the double doorway opening on the finely-furnished living room. "You have never been here before."

"No," she said, gazing around at the elegant furniture, the fine paintings and the huge chandelier that hung from the middle of the high ceiling. "This is a lovely old room."

"A trifle dusty," Barnabas said. "Hare is not a neat housekeeper. But I can't expect miracles from him."

Ann looked at him anxiously. "Have you seen John? He's vanished."

He shook his head. "No."

"I thought there was a bare chance he might have come here," she worried.

"He hasn't," Barnabas said. "He's likely somewhere in Collinwood. That house has forty rooms, not counting the cellar."

"William Collins may have been wrong," Ann said with a sigh. "He may not have left the house after all."

"That's probably the case," Barnabas said. "Sit down for a moment. I'd planned to go to Collinwood, but the constable came and kept me here."

"I won't stay long," she said as she settled down on one of the high-backed chairs of the candle-lit room. "I guessed something like that had happened."

"Would you care for a sherry?" Barnabas asked.

"Thank you."

He went to a side table where a decanter of the ruby-red wine and some glasses were set out. He poured out a glass and brought it to her. "Since you knew the constable was coming here you must also know why."

"I do," she said, taking the sherry. "And I'm sure you're not guilty."

He smiled sadly. "Thank you," he said. "I regret to tell you that I am."

She stared at him. "I don't believe it!"

"I must be honest with you," he said solemnly. "I meant that girl no harm. She was a silly creature and became very confused. The whole business was most unfortunate."

"What did the constable say?"

Barnabas made a careless gesture. "He warned me if anything of the sort happened again, I would no longer be welcome in Collinsport. It's a tune I've heard played before."

Ann was shocked. "Why did you do it?"

"That would take much too long to explain," he said quietly. "I could not help myself. Let it go at that."

"And what now?"

He smiled wearily. "If I were certain you were safe, I'd leave here at once. The time has come for me to go. But I hate to desert you in the midst of your trouble."

"Now the situation has become more complicated," she said. "I went down to the family cemetery today, and Simeon Hale turned up and seemed about to kill me!"

"Didn't you know he practically lives in that cemetery?"

"No. It was a surprise to me."

Barnabas looked bitter. "Susan is buried there. He makes a shrine of her grave."

"So I discovered," she said. "He took me over to it and started saying I should die."

"And then?"

"Quentin Collins came to my rescue!"

"Quentin!" Barnabas was astonished.

"Yes. So you see he occasionally does some good."

"That's hard to believe," he said.

"I felt the same way. In fact, I wasn't too nice to him because I had an idea he might be behind that scandal that's turned up. So in spite of the fact that he came to my aid, I was very cool to him."

"I approve of that," Barnabas said dryly.

"I was sure he was to blame for the attack on that girl, and had made it seem you were responsible so you'd be in trouble."

"Such a happening is not beyond possibility. But not this time."

"I sort of let him know I saw through his disguise, that I knew he was Quentin. And I hinted that some of the others have wondered about it," Ann went on.

Barnabas looked upset. "Did you tell anyone else?"

"No."

A look of relief crossed his face. "That is good," he said. "I don't want it revealed yet."

"I think I may have upset Quentin," she confessed. "It's hard to be sure. He conceals his feelings very well."

"What makes you think you worried him?"

"He at once began to talk of leaving," she said, "and he hadn't said anything about it before."

Barnabas listened with interest. "Perhaps it would be a good thing if he did leave. Then things would be that much less complicated."

"Eric saw us together."

"You and Quentin?"

"Yes. He was on the rooftop with a pair of binoculars. When I remarked about it later, he denied it at first. Then he admitted he'd been up there and acted very guilty."

Barnabas frowned. "I have warned you before about Eric."

"I know."

"There is something very wrong in that big house," Barnabas said. "And I think a great deal of it revolves around Eric."

Ann finished her sherry and stood up. "I really must go. I'm very concerned about John."

"Did Dr. Stair see him?"

"Yes, and he brought him some medicine tonight."

Barnabas looked sympathetic. "Perhaps the medicine will help."

"Now he's talking about not taking it," she said unhappily.

"Sometimes I don't know which way to turn."

"Meet the problem a single day at a time," Barnabas advised. "Otherwise you'll wind up with your own health wrecked."

She moved to the doorway. "If I didn't have you to confide in, it would be much worse. Please be more careful of yourself."

"If you're thinking about last night's episode, it's not liable to be repeated," he said. "At least not at once."

She studied him with bewildered eyes. "I wish I understood more."

"It's better this way," he said, and he touched his lips to her forehead in a brief kiss.

Once again the coldness of his lips startled her. Then he told her, "I'll see you as far as Collinwood."

The night seemed even darker than before, and Ann kept close to Barnabas. They said little as they walked along briskly, both occupied with their own thoughts. As they came close to Collinwood, she felt several more drops of rain.

Barnabas halted at the front door and smiled grimly. "If Eric is watching you this time, your reputation will really be in danger—being seen with me after my troubles of last night."

"I don't care what he sees," she said defiantly.

"I hope you find John in his room."

"I hope so."

"I'll see you tomorrow night, if not before," Barnabas promised. "And in the meanwhile, don't expose yourself to any more danger."

She smiled ruefully. "The trouble is I never seem to know where danger is."

"That's nearly always the case," Barnabas agreed. They said goodnight again and he waited until she was safely inside. She was still perturbed by his admission that he had attacked the village girl, although he had made it seem like a very harmless thing. She began to feel the other stories had been exaggerated. She still had complete faith in Barnabas, even if he did enjoy taunting the villagers by playing on their fears that he was a vampire.

No one appeared to be downstairs, so she went up the shadowed stairway to the second floor and then down the dark corridor to the door of the suite she and John were occupying. She'd barely reached her room when the storm broke with full fury. There was a sharp flash of lightning and then thunder rolled loudly over the great mansion. Seconds later the rain began to stream down. The storm was under way!

The door between her room and John's was shut. This was unusual and she walked over to it hurriedly and opened it. John was not in his room nor had he been in his bed. He must have gone out as William Collins had declared. But where? At once she was filled with new panic as all kinds of dreadful things flashed through her mind. Had he thrown himself from the cliffs? Or was he wandering, dazed, in the cemetery or the forest? Or even in the sinister swamp which Quentin had mentioned?

She went back to her room and quickly put on a rain cape and pulled its hood over her head. Then she rushed downstairs. As she reached the main floor, William Collins appeared from the direction of his study.

"You're not going out in this storm?" he asked.

"I must," she said. "John is missing!"

The old man frowned. "He didn't return?"

"No. I can't imagine what's happened to him, but he must be in trouble or he'd be here now." She moved towards the front door.

"Wait!" Mr. Collins came after her.

She turned. "Yes?"

"You mustn't go out on this awful night alone," he said. "Let me get Eric and some of the servants to help you in the search."

"Get help if you can," she said, "but I must start now. I can't bear to wait and worry about John." Without giving him any chance to argue further, she let herself out the front door and into the storm.

It was a wild night now. The thunder and lightning were sharp and the rain was coming down in torrents. Ann bent her head against the storm and started towards the cliffs. The lightning revealed the angry ocean and the roar of the waves made an eerie background sound whenever the other furies of the night subsided for a few seconds. In spite of her rain cape and hood, she was soaked through almost at once.

She staggered along the muddy cliff path, relying on the occasional flashes of lightning to see her way. It had been reckless of her to leave the house without a lantern, but she'd given way to her panic. Now she was alone in the storm without anything to help her, and without any clear idea of where John might be.

She stumbled and went dangerously near the edge of the cliff. Another foot to the left and she would have toppled to a sure death on the rocks far below. Advancing with more cautious steps, she strained to see ahead in the black, stormy night. And then she thought she saw someone far ahead, moving towards Widows' Hill.

She kept on and when the next flash of lightning lit up the sky, she clearly saw the walking figure again. It was a man and she was certain she'd found John at last. Sobbing her relief, she pushed herself to battle the driving rain and the ordeal of the thunder and lightning. But she could not cover the distance quickly.

All she could do was pray that John would be safe until she reached him. Then she'd somehow reason with him and coax him back to Collinwood. One thing she now knew: If she survived until the morning and was able to save John, they would both leave Collinwood at once. She could not continue in the gloomy mansion, where there were too many hazards for her sick husband. Tonight was the last straw. She knew how shell shock cases reacted to thunder and lightning. It was the same to them as being on the battlefield. John must be lost in the old nightmare of shellfire as he walked alone in the storm.

The lightning came vividly again and the thunder rolled and Ann saw the solitary figure of the man closer now. He was gazing out towards the ocean oblivious of the elements in such turmoil all around him. She was sobbing and panting for breath. If only John could survive the sound and fury until she was at his side. Then she could soothe his nerves and make him understand this was a storm and not a shellfire attack.

A hundred yards more! That was all. She felt better just knowing it. The lightning had not flashed for some minutes although the thunder rumbled ominously and the rain came down in sheets. Wet through and utterly weary, she stumbled on towards Widows' Hill and reached it just as the delayed lightning came to bathe the surroundings in an eerie blue blaze.

"John!" she called to her husband as she came near him.

He turned, and when she saw his face in the weird sustained blue light, she screamed wildly. For it wasn't the face of her husband that gazed malevolently at her, but that of the evil Simeon Hale!

She stood there frozen. "No!" she wailed.

He shouted something to her and then the darkness closed in on them again. Ann saw him lurch for her in the shadows and she turned to begin her flight back to Collinwood. This time she cut across the fields. Her terror gave her new energy. She didn't look back once but ran on, her heart pounding as if it must burst, and her chest aching beyond endurance.

She saw the shadow of Collinwood far ahead. It seemed such a long way off. And then she knew she could run no more and plunged forward in the deep wet grass, and lay there gasping. Each second she expected Simeon Hale to catch up with her. There was nothing she could do. Her strength was exhausted. The storm went on but she was barely conscious of it. She was weeping and she didn't even remember why!

Gradually she recovered a little, and she remembered where she was and why she had ventured out into this wild night. She had wanted to find John. Staggering to her feet, she began to slowly cover the rest of the distance to Collinwood. The storm still raged, but she was scarcely aware of it now.

She was very near the front entrance of Collinwood when she heard the low snarling noise to her right. Turning, she stared through the driving rain and saw the yellowish-gray monster of that other night crouching only twenty feet away from her, as if it might spring at her. Its burning amber eyes were bright with anger.

With a scream, she raced the final short distance to the front door of Collinwood and tried the handle. It was open and she stumbled inside. Both William Collins and Eric were there.

"You're back!" Mr. Collins said.

"The wolf! It's outside! On the lawn!" She gasped, still trying to catch her breath.

Eric said nothing but dashed across the hall into the den opposite the living room. A moment later she heard the sound of breaking glass and then a shot rang out. And a second one. As she and William Collins stood there in shocked surprise, Eric returned to them with a rifle in his hands.

"I remembered this was on the den wall and loaded," he said. "I think I managed to put a bullet in your monster-wolf!"

Ann heard no more because she'd slumped to the floor in a faint. When she opened her eyes she was on a divan in the living room. William Collins was standing over her anxiously.

"That's better," he said.

She stared at him. "I fainted."

"Yes. But that's no disgrace, considering what you'd gone through."

Memory returned to her and fear showed in her eyes. "Did Eric kill that creature?"

"He wounded it, and now a couple of the servants are out following its trail."

"They won't find it," she said wearily.

"That wouldn't surprise me," he said. "But Eric insisted on trying to catch up with the animal. He can be very determined."

She wasn't really listening. She was thinking of Quentin Collins and wondering if the monstrous wolf had been him or some other creature of the night. Was there any truth to the werewolf story? After tonight she couldn't dismiss it so easily.

"What about John?" she asked.

"No sign of him yet."

"Are you certain he went outside?" she asked. "Could he have wandered down to the cellars to escape the storm? Thunder and lightning drive him mad because of his shell shock."

Mr. Collins frowned. "I was sure I saw him go out the front door, but I may have been wrong. I'll see that a complete search is made."

She sat up. "Let me help."

"No," he said firmly. "You must go to bed, otherwise you'll be ill."

"I stand more risk of being ill if I don't find my husband," she told him firmly as she got to her feet.

"You're drenched," he said. "At least put on some dry things."

"No. As I am."

He stood beside her, thoroughly upset. "Where do you want to begin?"

She gave him a sharp glance. "Can you open that secret door in the closet of John's room? Do you know the location of the other hidden passages here?"

Collins looked concerned. "Yes. But he wouldn't be in there again."

"How can you be sure?"

"He doesn't know how to open the door."

"It may have been left open, as it was that other time, and then closed on him," she said accusingly. "He may be alone and frightened in one of those dark hidden passageways."

"Very well," he said with resignation. "I'll get a lantern."

She waited impatiently until he returned, certain that she was on the right track now. Barnabas had been the wise one. He'd told her he thought John was in the house rather than outside. She should have remembered that before becoming hysterical and rushing out into the storm.

William Collins returned with a lighted lantern in hand. "I think this is all going to be useless," he warned her.

"It's worth a try," she said stubbornly. As they started up the stairway, she said, "When I was out on the cliffs I ran into that Simeon Hale standing out there."

Mr. Collins looked grim. "That madman roams around here at all hours of the night and in every sort of weather!"

"Can't you do anything to stop him?"

"It seems not," he said.

They reached the second landing and went down the corridor to the door to the suite. Inside William Collins took the lead and went to John's bedroom and into the large closet. She stood a short distance behind him, watching as he groped futilely for the concealed spring that controlled the secret door.

"I can't seem to find it." He held the lantern up and scanned the wall.

"You must!"

"It should be here," he said, feeling the side of the closet wall carefully again.

Ann waited, knowing that they must not fail, and feeling almost certain that when that door was opened, they would find a terrified John standing on the other side of it.

William Collins gave a mild exclamation. "I think I have it," he told her.

She watched and saw the old man press firmly at a certain spot on the wall. As he did so the secret door swung open. But a wave of disappointment swept through her as she stared into the yawning darkness beyond, for there was no sign of her husband there.

CHAPTER 12

Illiam Collins turned to her with the lantern in hand, still reluctant to go on exploring the hidden passage. "I think this will be useless."

Ann had no thought of giving up. "I want to explore every inch of the secret areas."

He sighed. "As you say. Watch the steps—they are slippery and your shoes must be soaked."

"I'll be careful," she promised.

They descended the winding stone steps until they reached the cellars. Then, the old man leading, they followed the route she'd taken that other time. They entered the storage room with its ghostly stacks of discarded items, and even paused by the coffin in which she had been a prisoner.

"No one here," William Collins said, giving her a resigned look.

"Let us try the rest of the cellar," she said.

He shrugged and led her into the main cellar area. It was also lined with stored items. There was a huge coal bin near a furnace. Beyond that was a narrow passage that led to the wine cellar and a cold room for vegetables. They saw them all and still there was no sign of John Hayward.

Mr. Collins paused at the foot of the cellar stairs. "He's not down here," he said.

Ann refused to believe they had failed. "Are there any other secret areas?"

"Not that I'm aware of," he replied.

Ann felt he wasn't telling her the truth. "What about the attic?" She demanded. "We haven't looked there." On their way, they met Eric, who was just returning from his search. He was drenched, and looked more than annoyed.

"Did you have any luck?" his father asked.

Eric shook his head. "No. We followed the wolf down to the beach and lost track of him there."

"Did you go as far as Warren Miller's cottage?" Ann questioned.

Eric sounded surprised. "How did you know that?"

"I guessed you might have," she said.

"Yes. We did stop by Miller's cottage. We found the door open and the storm pounding into the place. All his things are gone. He's not there any longer."

"That doesn't surprise me," she said.

Eric said, "What about John?"

"We haven't found him yet either," Ann said.

Eric looked disgusted. "And you won't find him here. My father was right. He went out somewhere."

"Where?" she demanded.

"Who knows. The sensible thing to do is wait until morning."

"I can't do that," she protested. "You seem to forget my husband is a very ill man. That thunder and lightning storm is the last thing he should have been subjected to. It probably has sent him into one of his blackouts."

Eric looked gloomy. "I've had enough of the storm. Any more searching outside can wait until the morning."

"We can still check the attic rooms," she insisted, turning to Mr. Collins.

Eric gave his father a sharp look. "Are you going to do that?"

"She insists," he said with a sigh. "Let us go on up and get it over with."

Ann followed him up to the fourth floor. Eric had expressed his disinterest and left them to go to bed. Ann was beginning to lose heart though she didn't dare let on. If she didn't find John in the attic, there was nothing to do but wait until morning when it was light and the storm had ended. Then there would be a better chance of locating him.

But so many horrible things could happen to the sick man during the long, stormy night hours. It sickened her to imagine it. Now she quietly followed William Collins as they tried the various rooms off the attic hallways.

William Collins paused before a door near the end of the left wing. "This one is locked and I haven't got the key with me," he said. "It doesn't matter, since he couldn't get in there anyway."

She nodded to the door across from it. "What about in there?"

"Trunks and boxes in it," he told her. "But we'll take a look." He opened the door and stepped in and held the lantern up high. Then he gasped and turned to her, whitefaced. He blocked her from entering the room. "You don't want to go in there."

Fear streaked through her. "Why not?"

The old man struggled for words, his wizened face a study in distress. "It wouldn't be good for you."

Her eyes widened. "Is John in there?"

William Collins nodded as he still blocked her way.

"Let me go to him!" she cried.

"No use."

"He's not... " she left the question unfinished.

He swallowed hard. "He's hung himself," he said. "Looped a rope over one of the beams and hung himself!"

Ann passed out.

She was in her own room and Dr. Stair was standing by her bed. The gray dawn of another day was seeping in her window. She was in a kind of drugged bewilderment. Then the bitter memory of those last minutes in the attic returned.

She raised herself up in the bed. "John!"

The doctor eased her back on the pillow with a sober expression on his white-whiskered face. "That won't do any good," he said quietly.

Tears brimmed in her eyes. "Is it true?"

"I'm afraid so."

"He's really dead?"

"Yes."

She closed her eyes and moved her head painfully on the pillow. "It's my fault. I knew what the storm could do to him and I didn't reach him soon enough."

Dr. Stair spoke to her in a firm voice, "You must not blame yourself," he said. "That's wrong and it won't do anyone any good. John was doomed from the time of his war injuries. Sooner or later he was going to kill himself —or even you—or maybe you both. He was slowly losing his mind. The storm last night brought on a crisis. Luckily you weren't with him or you might not be alive at this minute."

The doctor went on talking in this vein and gradually Ann felt less guilty. She knew that all he said was true. She had been attempting to shut her eyes to the cold facts of John's condition, but that hadn't changed things. His mind had been cracking ever since they arrived at Collinwood. And though she hated to admit it, in her heart she knew he had tried to murder her. Better this way than that she should have to send him to a madhouse.

She looked up at the doctor. "I'll have to believe this was the best solution."

"I know it's shocking," Dr. Stair told her. "But at least he hurt no one but himself."

"He told me he didn't want to live here," she said. "He'd changed his mind about that. He wanted them to stop working on the house." She paused. "I'll have them finish it. But I'll sell it. There are too many bitter memories for me to think of remaining in Collinsport."

"That is something you can decide later," the doctor said.

"And I want to leave this house," she said. "Just as soon as I'm able. This house is cursed."

Dr. Stair nodded. "I've known others to say that. You can leave in a day or two. I'm sure they'll have a room for you at the hotel."

"I'd like to speak to Barnabas."

"I'll send a message to the other house," he said. "It's likely he'll come to visit you tonight."

"I don't want to remain in bed," she protested. "I want to look after the arrangements for John's funeral."

"William Collins has done that," the doctor told her. "And I order you to remain in bed, at least overnight. You must have this rest."

"But there are so many things to be looked after!" she said.

"If you do as I say, I'll let you get up and attend the funeral tomorrow afternoon," he said sternly. "If you disobey me, you may regret it. You are not as well as you think."

His firm manner impressed her. She knew that he was probably ordering what was best for her. "Very well, doctor," she said. "I'll do as you say."

"That's the sensible girl." He reached for his medical bag. "Now I'm going to give you something to make you sleep again."

By the time she woke again, it was mid-afternoon and the sun was coming in her window. She lay there, still fogged from the drugs. It seemed to her the tension had ended. Now it was merely a matter of her getting well, seeing John properly buried and then escaping from this shadowed house. She would remain in the village until the home they'd planned to live in was completed and then she'd sell it and leave the place forever.

But what about Barnabas?

Barnabas was important to her. She would like to see him again. Perhaps Barnabas might even play a role in her future. She was fond enough of him. If only he could solve his own problems! That was what might keep them apart. She would talk to him and maybe they could meet back in the London which they both knew so well.

These thoughts were drifting through her mind when the door of her bedroom opened and Eric came in. He looked pleased to see that she was awake.

"You've finished your sleep," he said, coming across to her bedside with a smile. "That's good. Dr. Stair thought you might sleep until the evening."

"I wish I had," she said faintly.

"You can't mean that," he reproached. "You can't give up your desire to live."

"I've lost most of it."

"That's a mistake," Eric said, taking one of her hands in his. "I realize John's suicide is a dreadful shock, but it has to be for the best. John was insane."

"Please!"

"I'm sorry," he apologized as she drew her hand from his. "I didn't mean to upset you. But you must admit he was very ill, with hardly any hope of recovery. You might have had him live on for years in some institution. At least this way it's over."

"Thank you for trying to make me feel better," she said wearily. "But I don't want to discuss it or even think about it."

"You shouldn't," Eric agreed. "You should think about the future. There are plenty of other men who'd consider themselves fortunate to get you for a wife. And I don't mind saying I'm one of them."

"Eric!" she protested.

"It's not the time or place for it," he said. "But I would like to marry you. I'd try to make you happy and it could give my life a meaning it hasn't got now."

Ann gave him a distressed look. It was hard to believe he could be so insensitive. She said, "Eric, I want to be alone. There are so many things I have to think out for myself."

"I'll go," he said. "But remember what I told you."

She wanted to change the subject. "Will the doctor be back?"

"He said he would but he didn't tell us when."

"Thank you," she said, closing her eyes.

Eric still remained at her bedside. "Is there anything I can do?"

"Go," she whispered. "Please, go."

This time he did leave. And in spite of the distress he'd caused her, she drifted off to sleep once again. When she awoke the next time it was night. There was a lighted lamp on her bedside table and Barnabas Collins was seated in a chair by her bed.

She sat up with a smile. "Barnabas!"

The man in the caped-coat grasped her gently by the arms. "Poor Ann," he said. "I'm so very sorry."

Her expression was plaintive. "So much has happened since we last met."

"Too much."

"Poor John," she said.

"He was headed for tragedy," Barnabas told her, his deep-set eyes full of sympathy.

"And Quentin has gone," she said. "Eric shot at a wolf who appeared on the grounds last night. He wounded it. And when he trailed it to the beach he came to Warren Miller's cottage and found it empty."

Barnabas nodded. "I have an idea Quentin was wounded. But I'm sure he's escaped with his life."

"They don't know it was Quentin."

"I don't think it matters. Let's leave it at that," Barnabas said.

"Perhaps it would be best," she agreed. "He did rescue me from that horrible Simeon Hale."

"True," Barnabas said.

"He was loitering on the cliff in the storm last night," she went on, "and he came after me. Luckily, I escaped him. But I'll always be in danger as long as I'm near him. Even though John is dead he'll transfer his need for vengeance to me."

"That is possible."

"So I plan to leave here," she said. "When the house is completed I'll go and never return."

"I think that wise," Barnabas said, his expression sad.

"What about you?"

"Me?"

"Yes. I would like to see you again. Perhaps we could become close friends. I've been thinking I want to return to London. And you spend a good deal of your time there, don't you?"

He nodded. "You're thinking of us meeting in London."

"Yes."

"It's a good thought," the handsome man said. "And maybe when all the unhappy matters here are settled it will be possible." He paused. "I wish I could spare you this, but I have some other unpleasant news for you."

She frowned. "What now?"

"About John and his suicide and about this house. I don't think John did kill himself. I have an idea he was strangled by someone and then it was made to appear like suicide."

Ann gasped. "Who would do such a thing?"

Barnabas glanced towards the hall door to make sure it was closed and no one could hear them. He bent close and in a low voice said, "For a long while I've been suspicious of Eric."

"Eric!"

"Yes," Barnabas said. "He is completely without character. I believe he is the one who made the attacks on you for which you have been blaming John."

These words brought new fear to her. She recalled the several times she'd discovered Eric spying on her and the hatred that had shown in his face. And that night when he'd followed her down the corridor...

She spoke in a near whisper, "Why?"

Barnabas looked puzzled. "I haven't been able to fathom a reason, unless he is insane also. But I've talked this over with Dr. Stair before coming here, and I think I have a plan to trap him."

"What sort of plan?"

"One which will require your help," Barnabas said. "Do you feel equal to it?"

"If he killed John he must be punished," she said. "What do I have to do?"

"Nothing but remain in this bed and pretend to be asleep. Dr. Stair is supposed to give you another sleeping potion tonight. But he won't. He'll give you plain water instead. I'm going to take up watch from the closet of what was John's room. Since Eric will expect you to be under drugs, it is my guess he will come to you here during the night. If so, I'll be ready for him."

She lay back against the pillow. "I thought it was over."

"After tonight it will be," Barnabas promised. "He'll either come to you or he won't. If he doesn't come we'll have to assume I'm wrong. If he does, we'll know that he has many things to explain."

"What about his father?"

"William Collins must be kept in the dark about this. I have an idea he knows what Eric has been up to and he's willing to protect him. Eric is all he has left now."

Ann stared up at him wanly. "I'll do my part," she said.

Barnabas bent and touched his cold lips to her cheek. "Good girl," he said. "And you needn't have any fear. I'll be close by to protect you."

He remained with her until the doctor came. Then he said goodnight. She had no idea how he planned to return to the other room. But she felt he probably was as aware of the secret entrances and passages of the old house as William Collins, if not more so. He'd know how to get back. Meanwhile, she had to play her game of pretence with Dr. Stair.

The doctor regarded her with a professional air. "You seem better," he said. "But to be sure, I'll give you another dose of sedative."

"I do want to sleep," she agreed, playing her part. While the doctor was preparing the sleeping potion for her, William Collins came into the room and Dr. Stair explained what he intended to do. He gave it great emphasis and Ann knew why: He was sure William Collins would pass the information on to Eric.

Mr. Collins came to the foot of her bed and gave her a paternal look of concern. "Obey the doctor's orders, my dear," he said. "We must get you safely through this."

"I intend to do everything he says," she agreed.

Dr. Stair came to her bedside with the glass of colorless liquid. "Drink this and you'll sleep until I return in the morning." He waited while she took the glass and drank it down.

Then both men left and she was in the room alone. The lamp had been turned low and the light was dim. Her heart began to pound and she wished she had taken a true sedative rather than just water. She wasn't sure her nerves were strong enough to see her through this final ordeal.

She partly closed her eyes and pretended to be asleep. She thought of John, whom she had loved so much, and she worried about whether Barnabas had managed to get back to the other room. She felt that he would be there, but there was always the possibility that plans could go wrong. Meanwhile, time passed and so far nothing had happened.

The clock on the dresser showed that it was after ten o'clock. She began to believe that Barnabas had been mistaken about Eric. If he was going to invade her room, he'd surely have come by now. Another twenty minutes went by. She was more nervous than ever.

Then she heard the handle of the door creak just a little as it was slowly turned. She held her breath and closed her eyes so that she had only a tiny slit to see through. The door opened an inch at a time, and finally revealed a pale Eric standing there with a mad, distorted look on his normally pleasant face.

The menace of his whole being terrified her. She watched as he closed the door softly. Then he came to her bedside one step at a time. His thin but powerful hands were ready to seize her throat as he bent over her.

But at that instant everything changed. Barnabas came in by the other door and threw himself on the surprised Eric. There was a struggle between them. Eric put up a grim battle. In the end, Barnabas struck him a powerful blow to the jaw that sent him to the carpet in a crumpled heap.

Barnabas, his brown hair wildly disarrayed, was breathing heavily. He turned to her with a knowing look. She was about to speak when she saw the door from the hallway slowly opening again. She cried out a warning, "Look!"

Barnabas turned just as another Eric came into the room. He quickly took in the situation and saw the body on the floor. He looked at them in despair.

"Now you know," he said simply.

"I've known for some time," Barnabas said quietly, as he pushed back the hair from his forehead. "I merely wanted to prove it."

Eric said, "What about Ann?"

"I'll tell her now," Barnabas said. Turning to her, he explained, "The man who invaded your room and who is on the floor now is Tom, Eric's twin brother."

"Tom!"

"Yes. He didn't die in Boston, as his father claimed. But he came out of his illness a dangerous lunatic. William Collins couldn't accept the sad fate that had overcome his favorite son, so he brought him back here under cover of darkness, and installed him in a secret room in the attic."

She listened with growing understanding. "Then it was Tom I saw from the attic window, not Eric. And it was Tom who chased me down the corridor and did all those other things."

Eric nodded sadly. "You're right. My father didn't intend that Tom should attack you or kill John. But it happened. Barnabas was the only one to guess. So now it means a mental hospital for my brother."

That was the climax of it all. They removed Tom, still unconscious, from the room, and Ann promised herself to try and forget the horror of those final minutes. William Collins came to her and abjectly asked a forgiveness she couldn't at once extend.

The next afternoon, she attended John's funeral and from the cemetery went directly to a hotel room in the village until the house was completed.

It was there that Barnabas came to see her a few nights later. He paced up and down before her as he said, "I must leave Collinsport before you do. I have no choice." He paused to face her. "I hope you understand. I don't mean to desert you."

"I'll manage," she said.

He smiled wanly. "No doubt Eric will ask you to marry him again. And maybe you should take his offer seriously. He's seemingly serious about reforming now that the fate of his twin brother has been decided. I believe he's going to turn out all right."

She shook her head. "I'll never marry Eric."

The handsome Britisher shrugged. "It was just a thought."

She stared up at him with worried eyes. "Are you going to be all right, Barnabas?"

"Yes. As long as I don't get involved in another mess with the town constable. By leaving here I'll avoid that."

Ann rose to go to him. "And we do have a rendezvous to keep in London."

"I'll not forget," he said quietly, taking her in his arms. "Just as I'll never forget you." He kissed her and then almost hastily said goodnight and went on his way.

The following day she received word that he had gone from Collinwood and the village. She hoped for word of him before the house was completed but it didn't come. And she left Collinsport with only the prospect of their eventual meeting in London to comfort her.

Carolyn had been listening raptly to the account of the frightened bride given her by her mother. Now she said, "Did you hear from Ann Hayward after she left the village?"

"Yes," Elizabeth said with a sad smile. "My mother received a number of letters from her. I would always look for the English stamps and know who the letters were from."

"What happened? Did she and Barnabas Collins marry?"

"No. They never met again."

Carolyn sighed. "I was afraid of that. Wasn't it awful for her?"

"From what my mother told me, Ann was very unhappy for a long while."

"I should think so," Carolyn said unhappily.

"She really loved Barnabas Collins."

"I could tell that," Carolyn said. "Did she die of a broken heart?"

Elizabeth laughed. "I think most of the young women who die of broken hearts are confined to the pages of the romantic stories you enjoy reading so much."

"Now you're making fun of me," her daughter pouted.

"Not really, I suppose it's nice that you have some romance in your nature. There's little of it around these days."

"What happened to Ann Hayward? You haven't told me."

"Well, she never came back to Collinsport," Elizabeth said. "But my mother wrote her regularly and told her all the news of the village. So she did know what was happening here."

"And?"

"She found herself a job in London doing welfare work and lived in a nice apartment. She didn't marry but seemed satisfied with her life. Perhaps she was hoping that one day Barnabas would return."

"You said he didn't."

"That's right," Carolyn's mother agreed. "Then the Second World War came along and once again Ann took up her army nursing career. Since we were also involved in the war, she saw many of our wounded boys. One day she walked into the room of a good-looking, gray-haired officer recovering from a leg wound whom she recognized at once as Eric Collins."

"Eric Collins!" Carolyn said delightedly. "What happened?"

"They renewed their friendship. He was very different from the brash young man she'd known twenty-five years earlier, just as she was more mature. It turned out that Eric had never married either and so for the second time Ann decided to marry one of her wounded American soldiers."

Carolyn jumped up. "So there was a real romance after all!"

Elizabeth nodded. "Indeed there was. The two of them lived happily in London after the war. Since then they've both died."

"That's sad," Carolyn said. "I wonder if our Barnabas Collins ever met them?"

"I suspect that he did," Elizabeth told her daughter with a gentle smile. "Barnabas has been a good friend to so many people."

COMING SOON:
BARNABAS, QUENTIN AND THE
SCORPIO CURSE

As the large bronze sports car with its white vinyl top sped swiftly along the road fringing the cliffs and overlooking the ocean on the left, Diana Collins had her first view of Collinwood in many years. The dark, sprawling old mansion perched high on the cliffs ahead brought back a rush of memories of her girlhood. She sighed deeply as she continued to stare at the big house. Her attractive oval face looked tense. She had black hair worn in pageboy style. She had often longed to return to Maine where she'd spent so many of her summer vacations with her sister, Carol, but she'd never dreamed it would be under such bizarre circumstances as these!

So many things had happened since her carefree holidays here with a distant cousin of her father's, Elizabeth Collins Stoddard. She recalled that Elizabeth had a daughter, Carolyn, who would probably now be in her late teens. Diana was twenty-three, and she had an idea Carolyn had been nine the summer eight years ago when they had spent their last summer vacation at Collinwood.

Pain showed in Diana's lovely gray eyes as she gazed out the window of the car. Since then her life had taken so many strange twists, so many unexpected, weird, and tragic things had happened it was hard to think of them as anything less than a nightmare, especially because lately, a black velvet curtain had been descending on her mind, blotting out memory and allowing her to behave in an uncontrolled and frightening manner. When consciousness returned after such a spell, she was left in an abject state of fear of her acts during the periods of her blackouts. And so she had returned to Collinwood this gray October day not for a happy vacation, but for medical treatment. For whether she dared to face reality or not, whether she allowed the words to cross her mind or not, the grim truth of it all remained. She was mad!

"We'll be seeing Elizabeth in a moment," her sister Carol said crisply from the wheel of the car. Blonde, excitingly lovely and eighteen months Diana's junior, her younger sister had taken over during this crisis. Carol was as coolly confident in managing the affairs of their father's estate as she was in driving this fast sports car. And she had even been willing to accompany Diana to Maine and stay with her at the private hospital while she underwent treatment for her mental illness. No sister could be more self-sacrificing than that.

Until just before her illness, Diana had gotten along well with Carol. Then there had been that unsettling incident involving Graham Weeds.

Graham was a young lawyer who had taken over their affairs after their father's tragic death in a private plane crash. Graham had also been engaged to Diana and then suddenly switched his affections to Carol. It had been a difficult situation for both girls, but Diana had attempted to give way gracefully to her younger and more vivacious sister. Only the onslaught of her madness at that time had given the crisis an ugly turn. But it was too late to worry about that now. There were so many other things to distress her.

Forcing her thoughts to one side, Diana said, "It's all so familiar!"

Carol slowed the car as they came to the driveway of Collinwood and gave her a worried glance. "You sound very strange. Are you feeling all right?"

Diana winced slightly. She knew Carol meant well with her concern for her, but if she could only be less blunt and a little kinder. But that was not her sister's nature. Sighing, she said in a small voice, "I'm all right."

"You don't sound it," Carol said suspiciously.

Diana became nervous, almost panicky. "It's just returning here again and remembering all those other good times."

Carol braked the car to a halt. "You're the sentimental one. I never cared for Collinwood all that much. I always felt angry that Dad didn't send us to some posh summer girls' camp. We were so isolated here!"

Diana frowned. "Elizabeth was always wonderful to us!"

"I don't deny that," Carol said, staring at her. "But I'd rather have been somewhere else."

Diana was about to ask her sister to make no reference to this when they saw Elizabeth. But before she could get around to saying this, the familiar figure of their relative appeared in the front doorway of the mansion.

"There's Elizabeth now!" Diana said with pleased excitement. She had always liked the attractive, dark-haired woman, and she was pleased to see that she had changed little in appearance over the years.

"Remember, we can't stay too long," Carol warned her. "We must check in at Dr. Meyer's before it's too late in the afternoon."

"I'll remember," Diana promised as they got out of the car.

Elizabeth welcomed her with a smile and a kiss. "Goodness, how you've grown," she said. And then she greeted Carol in the same way. "And so have you. You're both lovely young women and I've been remembering you as lanky-legged, awkward teenagers. Do come inside."

Diana went in first. The cool darkness of the reception hall of the old house was something she remembered well, as was the portrait of one of the Collins ancestors that hung there in a gold painted frame. The high ceilings and brooding silence of the ancient mansion had impressed her as a girl.

Elizabeth led them into the living room and waved them to places on a divan. A silver tea set and food were waiting on a tray on the table in front of them. Elizabeth sat herself down to preside over the tray.

"I wish Carolyn was here to meet you," she said. "But she's away at school in Brunswick. She'll be home for holidays, and you'll likely see her then."

"I hope so," Diana said. "She must be quite a young lady by this time."

Elizabeth smilingly agreed. "She is. And Roger is here, but he's at the plant in the village, and his son David is also away in boarding school. So I'm much alone in this big house these days."

Diana managed a forlorn smile. "As I remember the house from our holidays here, it's really immense. It has forty rooms, hasn't it?"

"You're always so peculiar about such things," Carol rebuked her with a scornful glance of her light-blue eyes. "Does it matter how many rooms? It's a big house."

Diana blushed. "I only said it because I remembered someone telling me the number of rooms."

Elizabeth at once came to her assistance. "You are right, Diana. The house does have exactly forty rooms." She smiled. "You both like tea, don't you?"

Carol nodded. "Yes. We mustn't stay too long. The doctor is expecting us."

Elizabeth was pouring out their tea. "Turnbridge House isn't far from here so it won't take you long when you leave. In fact, if you ever want to walk here, you can walk down the beach and save a good deal of time. It's much longer by the road." She handed them their cups.

"Is Turnbridge House as old as Collinwood?" Diana asked, anxious to make conversation that would pass the time pleasantly.

Elizabeth said, "No, but it is at least seventy years old. And of course it's a large, wooden structure with all kinds of wings and levels, the sort of old house it's easy to lose yourself in. It was empty for several years before Dr. Hugo Meyer came here and bought it for his clinic. I never dreamed Collinsport would become the headquarters for such a noted psychiatric clinic, but it has." She passed them the plates of sandwiches.

Carol asked, "How do the local people feel about having a mental hospital in the village? Do they resent it?"

Raising her eyebrows, Elizabeth said, "No. I don't think so. At least I've never heard any complaints. Many of the villagers are hardly aware of the clinic. Dr. Meyer only has a half-dozen or so patients at a time. I believe it is very difficult to be accepted for treatment there."

"Yes," Diana agreed quietly. "I'm very fortunate. I managed to get in. And he's even offered to provide another room for Carol and allow her to live there for at least a part of the time I'm a patient."

"That will be nice for you," Elizabeth said sympathetically.

Carol spoke up in her crisp way. "I didn't want to leave Diana alone. I'm not sure that Dr. Meyer can help her. I want to see if there is any daily improvement."

Elizabeth looked at Diana with concerned eyes. "I must say you don't look at all ill to me."

"Thank you," she said gratefully. At least she could be relieved that it didn't show.

Carol said, "Diana isn't at all well. Since Father's death she's had these blackouts. And when she comes to, she is never able to recall what she's been doing or anything else."

"Your father's tragic accident must have been a dreadful shock to both of you," Elizabeth said in a troubled voice. "Especially with your mother gone and having no other close relatives."

"It was a shocking blow," Diana said, a tremor in her voice at the memory of her father's kind face and the warm feeling of security she'd known when he was alive— a security lost to her now.

"I think that was what brought Diana's trouble to the crisis point," her sister said over her teacup. And then she added acidly, "Though you must know from your own memories of her that she was always on the nervous side."

"I didn't especially notice," Elizabeth said.

Diana gave her a faint, grateful smile. She could tell that Elizabeth felt sorry for her. She said, "I'm sure Dr. Meyer will be able to cure me."

"From all the accounts I've read of him, he's accomplished wonders in his field," Elizabeth agreed. "I'm sure you're doing right in placing yourself in his hands. I hear he has a new doctor on the staff. Someone from California, I understand."

"He has two doctors besides himself," Diana said.

"The other one would be Dr. Decker," the dark woman said. "I've met him several times. He's quite an elderly man and very German in looks and manner. I believe he came to this country after the Second World War."

Carol glanced at her wristwatch. "We'll really have to be on our way," she said. "What is Dr. Meyer like?"

"Gray, thin, and austere," Elizabeth said. "He demands strict discipline from himself, his staff, and his patients. I've heard a lot of inside talk about the clinic because by a strange twist of fate another member of a distant branch of the Collins family is also a patient there."

Diana was at once excited by the news. "That seems an incredible coincidence," she said.

"In a way, it is," the older woman agreed. "But this other party has been there for several months. Perhaps you've heard of him, although I'm sure you didn't meet him when you were here. He's from England, and his name is Barnabas Collins."

Diana at once recognized the name. "Isn't that portrait in the reception hall a study of Barnabas Collins?"

Elizabeth smiled. "A painting of his ancestor, the first Barnabas Collins, who left here and founded the English branch of the family nearly two centuries ago. And would you believe it? This young man bears a remarkable resemblance to the painting."

"What's wrong with him?" Carol asked.

Elizabeth said, "For a number of years he was unable to bear daylight. He remained in his home during the daylight hours, or at least inside if he happened to be traveling or living here at the old house. Both he and his father made a number of visits to the estate."

Carol in her brash way said, "And now he's crazy?"

Elizabeth looked displeased. "Not at all. He has overcome his reluctance to appear in the daylight hours, and he now feels he needs psychiatric help for the new life open to him so he won't revert to his former state. He comes over occasionally for a meal when the doctor allows him to leave Turnbridge. He is handsome and very pleasant. Both you girls will find him charming."

"He sounds very nice," Diana said, brightening. The news had cheered her for the first time in many days.

Her younger sister looked unimpressed. "There must surely be something wrong with him, or Dr. Meyer wouldn't accept him as a patient."

"He admits to having a problem," Elizabeth said. "But like most of the other patients being treated by the doctor, he is far from insane."

Carol gave Diana a significant glance. "Graham was right when he arranged to have you come here. From what Elizabeth says, it should be an ideal place for you."

Elizabeth smiled and quickly changed the subject by asking Diana, "Are you still as interested in astrology as you were?"

She returned the older woman's smile. "Definitely. I've gone much deeper into the subject."

"Interesting," the dark-haired woman said. "If I remember rightly you are a Scorpio."

"Yes," Diana said. "The Scorpion's symbol is really a serpent and not a scorpion. The serpent symbolizes both wisdom and evil."

"I think astrology is all a lot of nonsense," Carol said impatiently as she set her empty cup and saucer on the coffee table. "I blame Diana's being so absorbed by it as one of the reasons for her mental trouble."

Diana had heard this too often before. Now she reproached her sister, saying, "You know that's not so."

"I know nothing of the sort," Carol said coolly.

Elizabeth spoke up again, determined, it seemed, to handle the awkward situation with tact. "I'm sure the shock of her father's death and her own health condition has had more to do with Diana's troubles than any interest she may have shown in astrology."

Carol rose. "Perhaps so," she said. "Now we really must go."

Diana felt her sister was being too abrupt and giving little thanks to Elizabeth for the hospitality she'd shown them. She told her, "It was good of you to have us here. Now I feel more like going on to Turnbridge."

"It was a pleasure to see both of you girls again. When the doctor allows, you must come and visit me. And don't be concerned about your treatments. I'm sure Dr. Meyer will do wonders for you," Elizabeth said as she saw them out to the car.

As they drove away, Carol frowned. "I was glad to get away from there. Elizabeth goes on so about nothing."

Diana was staring out the side window at the calm blue water of the ocean. "I thought she was very nice to us."

"Oh, she was all right. But it has been too many years. We don't have a thing in common any more."

"I didn't feel that."

Carol rolled her eyes. "That doesn't surprise me. We seldom agree on anything. Maybe I shouldn't have come here. I should have let you do this on your own."

Diana felt a wave of uneasiness. "You know I want you with me," she said.

Carol sighed. "Sometimes I wonder. I have an idea you've never forgiven me for taking Graham from you. Actually, I didn't encourage him. It was his own idea."

Diana fought to keep from trembling. This was a subject she preferred to stay away from. She said, "People can't help falling in love. Graham found out he loved you rather than me. There's nothing to be done about it. Nothing to apologize for."

"But I know you're still in love with him!"

This was dangerously close to the truth. Diana gave her sister a despairing look. "I did care for Graham. Too much for my own good. But now I'm trying to forget that and consider him merely as a friend and a possible brother-in-law. It isn't easy for me yet. So I'd rather not talk about it."

"I'm sorry," Carol said. "I guess it worries me, too."

"It needn't. I want you and Graham to be happy."

They had come to a sign with the name "Turnbridge House" lettered on it, marking an opening in a stone fence. Carol expertly swung the sports car into the private roadway which wound down a hill. The roadway was flanked by trees on either side of it which gave it the shadowed feeling of a tunnel on this dark autumn afternoon. Moments later they came out to a parking area, a fairly good-sized lawn, and a great old-fashioned house of dark-stained cedar shingles with white window sashes and doors. It rose high in the air, and the large circular sunroom extending out over the cliffs promised a magnificent view.

Carol drove to the parking area and left the car beside a station wagon. Then they got out and started over to the entrance of the mansion, leaving their luggage in the car to pick up later. They were both rather tense as the meeting with Dr. Meyer drew near.

Reaching the paneled white entrance door, Carol pressed the ivory bell button and then gave Diana a wise glance as they waited. "It looks isolated enough," she said.

"It does," Diana said with a tiny shudder rippling through her. Not only was she nervous about meeting the doctor, but the brooding mansion depressed her. For no reason she could pinpoint she felt it might harbor evil beyond her understanding.

"I suppose Dr. Meyer needs a quiet spot to look after his loonies," Carol said with a look of disdain on her beautifully chiseled face. It was a remark typical of her callousness.

There was the sound of movement on the other side of the door and then it was opened by a bent, elderly man in the white jacket of a doctor. "Yes?" he enquired with a hint of guttural accent.

"I'm Carol Collins," her sister said. "And this is my sister, Diana, who is to register here as a patient."

The elderly doctor at once showed a smile revealing the shining falseness of his too-even, ill-fitting teeth. "Yes, of course," he said. "We were expecting you two young ladies." He had a narrow, thin face and his jacket and shirt seemed too large for his shrunken figure. His head was bald except for patches of short gray hairs above the ears, and his eyes were a faded blue behind thick rimless glasses. "I'm Dr. Max Decker, senior associate of Dr. Meyer," he said with noticeable pride.

"We've heard about you, Doctor," Carol said. "What should we do first? Our bags are in the car."

"I'll have one of the servants get them and take them upstairs to your rooms if you'll give me the car keys," he said. "And while this is being done you can have your first interview with Dr. Meyer. He is waiting in his office for you."

Carol gave him the car keys and told him which bags were hers and which belonged to Diana so they could be placed in the proper rooms. Then they followed him down a long hallway to the rear of the house. There on the lower floor they found Dr. Hugo Meyer in his office. The thin, gray-haired man rose from his desk to greet them. There was an air of melancholy distinction about his stern, lean features. Diana recognized him from photographs she'd seen in various publications. His unorthodox approach to mental therapy had received a lot of attention.

"Which of you two young ladies is to be my patient?" was his first question. They were at once introduced to the eminent medical man by the elderly Dr. Decker, who then vanished from the book-lined office whose windows overlooked the bay.

Dr. Hugo Meyer stood staring hard at Diana. "So you feel I will be able to help you?" he asked in his slightly nasal voice.

"Yes," she said quietly.

"We had better have our first talk," he said. He gave Carol a sharp glance. "This will be a private conversation between your sister and me," he explained. "I would suggest you go on to your room and unpack. Dr. Decker will show you where it is."

Carol hesitated, her brashness leaving her as she regarded the medical man with some awe. "Perhaps my sister would prefer that I remain," she said. "I've come here to support her in any way I can."

Dr. Meyer looked bleak. "You cannot remain here under any circumstances. I have only allowed you to come here after serious consideration. It may be that I'll decide you'll have to leave in the interests of your sister's health. We shall see. Meanwhile, please go."

Diana told her. "It will be all right."

"Very well," Carol said uncertainly. "I'll be upstairs."

Dr. Meyer closed the door after her and then turning to Diana waved her to a chair placed before his desk. He moved to a position facing her and said, "I have read all the details of your case, and it interests me a good deal."

"Thank you," she said.

"These blackouts of yours. How long do they usually last?"

"Generally only a few minutes," she said, her cheeks burning. She was always embarrassed when it came to discussing this dread weakness. "But there have been times when they've gone on for nearly an hour."

"During that time you're in what might be described as a sleepwalking state?"

"I suppose that does describe my condition," she agreed in a troubled voice. "The awful part is that I do things and then have no memory of them when I come out of the spells."

He nodded grimly. "Since your father's death the attacks have gotten worse?"

"They didn't really begin until then," she said, her face lined with worry. "As a girl I was given to sudden fainting fits, but they didn't last more than a moment or so."

"So your history of blackouts does go back to childhood?"

"I suppose so. But those spells were very short, and they only happened when I was very upset and nervous."

Dr. Meyer had picked up a file from his desk and opened it. He was now studying some of the papers. "We can safely say that beginning with your father's fatal plane accident, these spells hit you with a new intensity?"

"Yes."

"Complicated by the loss of your fiance to your sister?"

She was blushing furiously now. "I suppose so. But it wasn't their fault. They are both fond of me. Neither of them would want to hurt me. They just fell in love. And they still have guilt feelings about what has happened. That is probably the main reason Graham Weeds worked so hard to have you accept me for treatment and why my sister felt it her responsibility to come here with me."

The doctor gave her another of his penetrating glances. "You have no hatred for either of them because of what happened?"

In a small voice, she said, ""No."

His sharp gray eyes were focused on her. "So it might be sublimated feelings of hatred and frustration which have brought you to the state you're in?"

"I don't think so," she faltered. "I hope not."

His eyes never left her. "According to the report I have here, there was an attack made on this Graham Weeds by you during one of your blackouts."

"Yes," she said faintly.

"You stabbed him when your blacked-out mind had lost some of the normal restraints! Doesn't that suggest something—that you are being torn by your resentment of what happened?"

She looked down. "I suppose so. I don't know. I can't remember any of it!"

"Yet your sister found the young lawyer on the floor bleeding from a knife wound in his side while you stood over him in a dazed state. Had she not quickly called an ambulance, he would have surely died."

"Yes! Yes!" she cried frantically. "Don't go over it, please! Don't make me think about it!"

"I'm sorry," the doctor said. "But making you think about it may be an important step in my attempting to cure you."

Diana clasped her hands over her face. "All I want to do is forget what happened and live peacefully."

"I trust you may be able to do that before long, but it will take time and treatment," the doctor said.

"Anything to be well again!"

"Exactly," Dr. Hugo Meyer said, putting down the file. "We will begin your treatments tomorrow. I understand from your file that you are a Scorpio and have a strong interest in astrology."

"Yes," she said, expecting him to disapprove.

Instead, he offered her the ghost of a smile. "I'm a believer in the stars myself. And I also happen to have been born a Scorpio."

His revelation both pleased and startled her. She had been expecting him to condemn her interest in the stars, as Carol so frequently did. Instead, he seemed ready to discuss her exciting hobby with her.

She said, "I was afraid you'd not understand."

"But I do," he assured her. "We must talk about astrology later. When I know more about the particular time of your birth and the influences bearing on you at that moment, I'll understand you better." He paused. "We have few restraints here. You'll meet the other patients in the dining room. We demand certain undertakings from you. But you'll become familiar with all those things in time. I'm not sure that your sister is going to fit in. We've never had a mere paying guest before. And we cannot keep her here if she upsets any of the others."

"That is only fair," she said, remembering that in the beginning she'd wanted Carol with her. Perhaps Carol had really made her believe that she should have some kind of company, and so she'd gone along with the unorthodox idea. Now she no longer cared. Perhaps if the truth were to be told, she would prefer that the doctor order Carol to return home.

"This old house is a place of legend and mystery much the same as Collinwood, with which you're familiar, I believe."

"Yes. I am."

"You'll find this house has many similarities to Collinwood though different in structure. These are the lands of places in which you picture phantoms lurking in every corner. And yet it has proved ideal for my clinic." He nodded to indicate the interview was at an end. "Now you may go to your room. I'll see that you meet the others at dinner."

The distinguished doctor showed her to the door and told her how to get to the front of the house and the stairway leading up to her room, then left her on her own. She moved along the dark, shadowed hallway nervously wondering which floor her room would be on and whether it might be close to Carol's.

She was trying to decide what her opinion of Dr. Meyer was when suddenly out of the shadows a weird figure gradually took shape before her. A tall, broad male figure was coming toward her and she was at once filled with a chilling fear. Before her terrified eyes a bizarre face loomed closer to her. The newcomer had a shaved bald head, was youngish and not bad-looking, but his eyes were what made her tremble. There was a cruel light of madness in them.

Diana halted.

The man glared at her in the semi-darkness. Then he savagely seized her by the wrist. She drew back with a cry of fear, certain she was confronted by a lunatic, and frantic to escape his grasp!

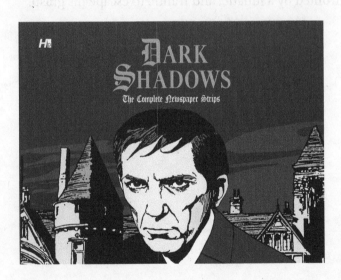